MEET ME IN THE CAFÉ AROUND THE CORNER

VIRGINIA COLLIER

ISBN: 978-1-915164-31-5 (Paperback)
       978-1-915164-32-2 (Ebook)

Published by:
      Maple Publishers
      1 Brunel Way,
      Slough,
      SL1 1FQ, UK
      www.maplepublishers.com

CONTENTS

CHAPTER ONE

Just as Sylvia was about to leave the house the clock struck 07:30am. As usual she was late in catching the bus for work.

Sylvia worked for a company that made parts for motor cars. In the Second World War the factory made parts for aeroplanes and tanks, that sort of thing. As it was only seven years since the war ended, things were still raw for most folk especially the ones who served their country.

Sylvia lived in Manchester, a few miles from the town Centre. She usually took the bus into work with her best friend Bridget, who lived over the road from her.

Sylvia was a bright, pretty lass with blonde hair that she put in a bun when at work. Sylvia would often dream for something exciting to happen in her life instead of working in a factory all day.

As Sylvia approached the bus stop, she could see her friend already waiting. Bridget was a pretty brunette with a witty nature who took every day as it came. Sylvia and Bridget were very close; no matter what was happening, they were always there for each other. Even if one of them was wrong.

It was a short bus ride to the All Parts factory. Sylvia had been working there for nearly two years, and Bridget just a little bit less. They both sorted the wages out every week.

"Bus is late this morning," Sylvia said while hunting through her bag for some change to give the bus driver. "That'll mean Brian will be on our case again for being late."

Brian was only their supervisor, so if anyone did anything wrong, he would go running to the Manager.

After waiting a short while, chatting about nothing overly important, the bus showed up. "About time!" Sylvia moaned as she stepped onto the bus. "This is the second time this week the bus has been late. I've a good mind to phone the depot and give them a piece of my mind," Bridget says as she lights a cigarette.

Sylvia and Bridget liked working at the factory as it was a Monday to Friday job. That meant they had the weekends to themselves. Mostly Sylvia and Bridget would go to the Crystal Rooms as they loved the dancing. Most folk would end up there at the end of the evening.

Bridget was a hopeless romantic who wore her heart on her sleeve. Being only twenty it was boys, and Sylvia going to the pubs. Living in Manchester was never dull: there were plenty of things to do and, since the war, it was as though everyone was still in celebration mode.

As the bus rolled to a stop they could hear the horn blow for all the workers to get to their work stations.

"Hurry up Sylvia, else Brian will really be on our case again."

"Oh, I'm not scared of him," Sylvia replied with a wave of her hand.

"You'll change your mind when he docks our pay."

When Sylvia and Bridget got to the bottom of the stairs. They could see Brian above them, waiting. "You're late! I will be docking your pay if you are late again. Get to work!"

As Sylvia passed Brian, she could feel her temper begin to boil. She knew it would do no good to say anything Brian would only go straight to the manager's office. You see, Brian's sister Joyce was the manager's wife.

"Hello ladies. Late again I see."

"Not you an all, don't start Johnny!"

"Hey! I'm on your side remember?" Sylvia smiled as she knew Johnny was only joking. You see, Johnny was really a nice bloke, good looking and charming, with slick, black hair and blue eyes. He would always be the one to sort out any problem that would arise. Johnny was one of them in the office who dealt with the invoices.

Ken, who was in his forties and mostly got on with everyone, was in charge of the shipping, making sure the deliveries got to the right places. Then there was Vera: a middle-aged woman who kept to herself most of the time. She was in charge of all of the orders: a very important job in the company. As All Parts ordered different metals from all over the world, they would have deliveries almost every day.

The office itself had two large windows, which let in a lot of light. Even though it was quite a small room. There were six offices all around the same size. They all had a desk, which made it feel like being back at school; and even with the large windows, it still got stuffy throughout the year.

Glancing at the clock, Bridget nudged Sylvia. It was ten thirty, and time for a tea break. Sylvia got up and reminded Brian that it was time for a tea break. He sighed and glanced at his watch, "I suppose it is. Take a fifteen-minute break."

With that, everyone hurried to go to the toilet before Brian called them all back to their desks. Mostly they would take it in turns to make the tea. Today it was Bridget's turn. Bridget never liked making the tea, as Creepy Brian would always be hovering around. Once everyone had their drinks, they would sit on the chairs nearest the door to get a cool breeze from outside.

"Not a bad cup of tea if I say so myself." Johnny always says that when either Sylvia or Bridget makes the tea.

"It's not fair Brian never gives us chance to go to the toilet and have a cuppa," Bridget complained, whilst giving Brian a snide stare. "No wonder he's single. No one wants to put up with him."

"Time to get back to work, you have had plenty of time to finish your drink," Brian shouted to everyone and on that order, they went back to work.

CHAPTER TWO

"How are you getting on with the order, Alfie?" Sid asked.

"I'll finish it by home time." Alfie shouted with a wink.

Everyone got on with Sid even though he was the supervisor. It was difficult not to like him: he was a hardworking, likeable soul who would do anything to help someone who was struggling.

Alfie was one of the hardest workers. He always had the most parts made each day, with it being piece work. The more parts made, the better your wage packet was at the end of the week. With Alfie having two kids to feed, it was an extra bonus.

Most of the folk in the factory worked hard for their pay and, even though it was hard work, most of them liked working at All Parts. It helped that pretty much all of the staff got on well with each other.

There was a cry of frustration from the corner of the floor and Gilbert shouted Sid over. "This machine's been playing up all morning. I can't deal with it anymore."

"I'll get an engineer out as soon as I can, it should be fixed by lunch time."

As soon as the lunch bell rang, everyone rushed away from their stations toward the canteen where they formed an orderly queue. The owners of All Parts provided all the workers with a free meal each day. Not all companies would do that. Doris and Karen were the cooks in the canteen and would cook good, homemade food for Sara to plate up for the workers. After everyone had finished their meal, some would go outside for a cigarette while sally cleared the canteen, then it was time for everyone else to go back to work.

When the canteen was cleared away, Doris and the others would sit down to have their lunch. Doris was the one in charge, but she never pulled rank on the other girls in the kitchen. Sara and Sally were the young ones and all they talked about was boys and what they had been up to over the weekend.

CHAPTER THREE

After everyone had eaten their lunch, they all had a wave of energy to work the rest of the day. Annie, Mable and Wilma were packers, and they were quick at packing the small parts, chatting away as they went along.

"Are you going to the cinema tonight?" Annie asked Wilma as she packed a box.

"I may come, what's on tonight?" Wilma asked.

"Robert Taylor is on in *Above and Beyond.*"

"I love Robert Taylor!" Wilma gasped.

"It starts at 7 o'clock at the Majestic. I can meet you outside at 6.30pm?" Wilma agreed with a faint smile while she carried on packing.

"Not long now 'till home time." Annie glanced at the clock, then turned to face Wilma and spoke. "It is really hot in here today," she said as she wiped her brow. "Can't wait to get out of here."

A while later, Annie nearly forgot to tell Wilma and Mable that Alfie had told her earlier that day that there was trouble brewing in one of the offices. Wilma and Mable both stared at Annie, waiting for her to tell the rest of the story. After a pause Annie continued. "Well, as the story goes, everyone in the office has it in for Brian."

"What you mean *have it in for Brian*?" Wilma and Mable were waiting for an answer.

"Apparently, Brian makes everyone in the office wait when the bell goes at home time."

"Why does he do that?" Mable asked.

"Well, it all started when Brian accused Bridget Molt of tampering with the wages. That was only a few months after Bridget started working here. She was in tears about it. The manager looked into it but nothing else was said about it." Brian makes them wait when the bell goes like children at school. Just to make a point, I suppose."

"Everyone knows that Brian is nothing but a sneaky weasel, running to the manager about any little thing. I bet the manager is fed up with him. Good job we haven't got Brian out here with us." Annie, Mable and Wilma laughed has they carried on working.

CHAPTER FOUR

After most of the workers had left the factory, Sid was alone on the factory floor checking how many parts the workers had done that day. Suddenly, someone came up behind. "Have you decided what you are going to do now?"

Sid spun around and came face-to-face with Brian. For the last six months Sid had been sneaking parts out and selling them on the black market. Things had been tough at home, with a wife and three kids to feed, money was tight.

Brian had found out, about two months ago and decided to black mail Sid. He had been having his cut out of what Sid had been getting for the parts. "I want more than you're giving me," Brian said angrily. "Or do you want me to have a word with your manager?"

Brian had Sid where he wanted him. The problem Sid had was that if he gave Brian any more money, it wouldn't be worth taking the parts in the first place. Anyhow, he'd decided he'd had enough, he wanted a clean slate before it was too late. He'd realised that if he got caught, he could get the sack or maybe even go to prison! Then his wife Suzi and the kids would have it even harder, with no money coming in.

Brian knew just how to play him. Sid felt trapped, like a wild animal that had been caught and locked in a cage. He knew he would have to continue with the deed.

"Well? Where is my cut for this month?" Brian asked angrily.

Sid started to lose his temper. "I haven't got the money yet; I need more time." The more Brian kept on at him, the more Sid wanted to hit him. Sid knew he had to calm down before he did lose his patience with him. He knew he had to do something soon before it got out of hand. With Brian wanting more money, Sid wished he hadn't started selling the parts in the first place. All he wanted now was Brian gone.

CHAPTER FIVE

Sylvia glanced at the clock for the eighth time. Just an hour to go before home time.

It was early April, and the nights were starting to draw out, so it was light when everyone left work.

When Sylvia finished for the day, Johnny hissed to get her attention. "Are you going to the Majestic tonight?" Johnny asked quietly, while Brian was busy putting files away.

Before Sylvia could answer Johnny, Brian shouted over to her. "These files are a disgrace; you can stay behind and get them in order!"

Sylvia could feel her face go red. Filled with anger she knew she had to keep calm and to not give him any cheek back. She knew that, if she did, Brian would be more than happy to give her the sack.

When the bell went for home time, Johnny whispered to Sylvia that he would stay behind to help her with the files.

Sylvia smiled then told Johnny, "It is best that I do

the files on my own. I don't want to get you in trouble as well."

"He can't get away with treating you like this," Bridget said angrily. "I will wait for you in the café around the corner."

Sylvia gave a faint smile then said to Johnny, "Yes I will go to the Majestic tonight." Johnny turned to Bridget to ask if she was also coming.

"Try stopping me." Bridget, Sylvia and Johnny would often go to the cinema in the week.

When everyone left the office, it was just Sylvia and Brian. "It won't take long to get the files in order, half an hour I would say." Brian sniggered as he sat down at his desk, watching Sylvia's every move. As she put the files in order, she could feel the hatred towards Brian grow stronger, as she knew too well that Brian had mixed the files up on purpose so he could make her stay behind and put them back in order. This was the last straw for Sylvia.

You see this wasn't the first time Brian had made Sylvia stay behind. The last time he had made her stay behind was because she forgot to make him a cup of tea.

Sylvia knew it was a waste of time complaining to the manager as Brian knew he had you where he wanted.

"I've finished with the files, Mr Dent."

Brian slowly got up from his chair. He glanced at Sylvia then the files. "I suppose they will do." Then Brian suddenly grabbed her. Still sniggering, he moved his hand down to Sylvia's crotch. Sylvia was in complete shock, but she managed to pull herself together enough to push his hand away. For a slight moment she felt like she was frozen in time. With everything Sylvia had, she pushed Brian out of the way, grabbed her bag and hurried out of the office.

When Sylvia was out of the factory, she broke down and cried. She must have been in shock: it almost felt like it had happened to someone else. She couldn't believe that Brian did that to her. He had never tried to sexually assault her before; in all the time she had worked at All Parts.

Walking to the café, Sylvia was in some sort of trance, like she was sleep walking or high on something. When she reached the door of the café, she could see Bridget waving for her to come and sit by her.

"Shall I get you a drink, do you want a coffee?"

Sylvia did not answer straight away, and Bridget asked her again. "Yes, a coffee will be fine." Bridget frowned, unsure why Sylvia was acting strange, but went to get her a coffee without asking any questions.

When Bridget returned with a coffee, Sylvia was crying. Bridget quickly sat down beside her and asked, "Whatever is the matter?"

Sylvia blew her nose with a tissue then quietly said, "Brian." That is all she could manage to say.

"Whatever has that piece of shit done this time?" Sylvia remained silent. Then Bridget asked again. "Tell me Sylvia."

"It was Brian." She was finding it hard to get the words out. "He grabbed me and put his hand on... you know... below." Bridget's face changed when she knew what that creep had done.

"That creep needs to pay for what he has done to you." By now Bridget was fuming. Even though Brian hadn't sexually assaulted Sylvia before, he had in fact caused problems with her in the office.

It all started when Brian asked her out on a date, which was about two months ago. Sylvia said she did not want to go out with him but thanked him for asking. Everything seemed to be all right after, but then Brian started picking on Sylvia for any little thing.

After Sylvia finished her coffee she said to Bridget, "Let's go before we miss the next bus home." While they were waiting for the bus, Sylvia decided never to mention what happened in the office again.

"We better hurry up and have our tea before we go to the Majestic with Johnny." Bridget was surprised that Sylvia wanted to go to the cinema after what happened. As they walked home from the bus stop, neither of them spoke until they reached Bridget's house. "Well, I will see you in an hour then?" Sylvia glanced at Bridget, but her thoughts were somewhere else.

After Sylvia left Bridget, she arrived home and went straight up to her bedroom. She did not want her Mum and Dad to see her upset. She sat on her bed, her mind going over what happened earlier. It felt more and more like a scary dream that happened to someone else. Sylvia knew something had to be done to make Brian pay for what he had done to her. He had gone too far this time.

After thinking things over, Sylvia went downstairs to have her tea before getting ready to go to the cinema.

After Sylvia had finished her tea, she made her way

back up to her bedroom to get ready to meet Bridget and Johnny. Even though she knew Brian had to pay for assaulting her, she was scared Brian would make out that she was lying about the assault. He knew just what to say and she could end up losing her job if they believe Brian over her.

When it was 6.30pm, Sylvia was more than ready to leave the house. As she approached the end of the road, she could see Bridget waiting. Sylvia was glad she had Bridget for a friend; she had been there for her since they were kids.

When Sylvia reached Bridget, she told her she had decided to report Brian to the manager in the morning. At least she had Bridget and Johnny for support. Sylvia wanted it to end once and for all. Even if she lost her job, she did not care anymore. She was feeling positive about her plans to deal with Brian and was starting to feel more like her usual self.

When she told Bridget what she was going to do. Bridget hugged her. Sylvia knew then that she was doing the right thing. The only one to tell now was Johnny. She thought he would know what to do.

On the bus ride Sylvia and Bridget spoke about the film they were going to see at the Majestic and how they both loved the handsome star, Robert Taylor.

When the bus reached their stop, they both jumped off. After pausing to light a cigarette, they spotted Johnny coming up the road. "On time as usual" Bridget grinned.

In a strange way Sylvia was pleased to see Johnny, he had been a good friend to her and Bridget, since he started at All parts two years ago. He always had their back when they needed him.

Johnny would always pay for the cinema tickets, he would say "If I can't treat my ladies then there's no point in it all."

As the three of them walked through the doors of the theatre Bridget said, "I'm just going to freshen up." It was clear to Sylvia that Bridget was giving her time to talk to Johnny about Brian. Sylvia knew if she didn't tell him now, she may bottle it.

After Sylvia told Johnny everything, he just looked at her, thinking she was joking. It was clear by the look on her face that she was serious.

Johnny began to get angry. "That spineless shit, wait till I get hold of him tomorrow!"

"No, let's be rational and not lose our jobs over him."

It was clear he wasn't happy about it, but Johnny knew Sylvia was right. Just then Bridget returned, she could see by Johnny's face Sylvia had told him everything. "If he ever hurts you or Bridget again, so help me I will kill him."

Bridget and Sylvia had to calm Johnny down before they went in to see the film. Sylvia was hoping everything would be clearer by the morning.

CHAPTER SIX

The next morning was a beautiful sunny day, much too nice to be stuck in a factory. As soon as the bell went all the workers made their way into the factory.

Not long after, Annie, Wilma and Mable started chatting about the film they went to see at the Majestic, the night before. One of the older ladies asked Annie if she had heard the news.

"What news is that Martha?" Annie asked.

"Well didn't you see the police cars out at the front gates?"

"Oh yes, I did now you mention it, Martha."

"What has happened?" Wilma asked.

"You will never believe what has happened" Martha eager to tell them. "It is Brian Dent from the office, creepy Brian."

"Oh, God, not him. What's he done this time?" Annie moaned, thinking he had sacked someone or something.

"Well, he was found dead late last night."

"What?" Annie, Wilma and Mable stopped in their tracks! "You're having us on, who told you that?"

"It was Bill Mills the caretaker who found him. He was found in the manager's office, he told me in the café, around the corner before I got in this morning. He told me he was the one who called the Police, early this morning. Bill had to stay by the body 'till the police came."

"Do the police know how he died?" Annie quizzed.

"Bill didn't know. The police won't say until they do a post-mortem. Apparently, the police will be giving interviews throughout the day. Bill did think it was strange that Brian was in the Manager's office, as it is usually locked after the Manager has gone home. Also, the last time Bill had checked the Managers office was 12 o'clock. Brian must have had a key to get in as the lock wasn't broken. The killer must have taken the key with them."

"How often does Bill check the rooms?" Annie eagerly awaited the answer, her mind going a mile a minute.

"Bill told me that he is supposed to check the offices every two hours, in case there is a break in. Brian must have been murdered after 12 o'clock."

"Blind me, I can't believe something like that has happened here. It was only yesterday we were slating Creepy Brian. It must have brought him bad luck I would say. Who would have thought it?"

Annie was still in shock from it all.

CHAPTER SEVEN

As Doctor Bentley was looking over the body, he could see there was a substantial amount of blood indicating he was killed where he was. When the body was turned over, Doctor Bentley could see there was a wound to the chest area. Either a stab or bullet wound.

The deceased had short, brown cropped hair and was wearing navy blue trousers, a black jumper and black shoes with a gold signet ring on his right hand.

By the deceased was found, one rubber glove and one torch. Doctor Bentley said he would know more after the post-mortem, that following day. After dusting for fingerprints, the body was ready to be moved. At this point, PC Lamb - one of the first officers on the scene - informed Inspector Wright that Mr Bill Mills had in fact seen someone running from the back entrance of the factory, but couldn't quite see if it was a man or a woman as it was pitch black. "He said it was about 12:55am, Gov."

With this new information and after speaking to the

doctor, Inspector Wright and PC Lamb had the body moved to the mortuary.

Inspector Wright had recently moved to Manchester with his wife and baby daughter from Scotland Yard London. This was in fact his second case in Manchester. His first job was to speak to the manager, Mr Roger Mortimer, in the office next door. The Inspector was a tall man with blonde cropped hair with blue eyes. He was a fair man who liked to get things done right.

Mr Mortimer was still in shock. It seemed so much more surreal that it was his brother-in-law who had been found. When PC Lamb brought Mr Mortimer in for questioning. He was asked to take a seat.

"I know it's been a shock for you, Mr Mortimer, but when was the last time you saw Mr Dent?" Inspector Wright looked straight at Mr Mortimer, without breaking eye contact.

"Well, it must have been around 5.30pm when I left the factory." Brian had come to my office as he had some paperwork for me to sign before I left to go home. I never saw him again."

"Would you say it was exactly 5.30pm, Mr Mortimer?"

"I would say exactly 5.30pm. I did come back to my office around 10.30pm as I forgot some paperwork I needed completing for the next day. The only person I saw that night was the caretaker. I said good night to him then I left the factory to go home."

"Mr Mortimer, do you know why Mr Dent was in your office when he was killed?"

"Well, he does have a key in case I am off work

poorly or away on business. I don't know why he was in there last night."

Inspector Wright pushed further. "Lastly do you know anyone who wished Mr Dent dead?"

"Well can I be frank with you, Inspector?"

"Yes, by all means Mr Mortimer?"

"I have to say everyone who knew him, despised him."

"You say everyone?" Inspector Wright was now intrigued as to what Mr Mortimer meant by that comment.

"Well, that might be a bit much to say everyone. Most of the folk in his office did."

The Inspector was surprised by Mr Mortimer's answer. "Right, I think that will be all for now"

After showing Mr Mortimer out of the office, the Inspector decided to question the rest of the office workers. He asked PC Lamb to bring Miss Bridget Molt in next.

When Miss Molt entered the office, the Inspector then asked Miss Molt to take a seat on the other side of the desk in front of him. "I just want to ask you a few questions. When was the last time you saw Mr Dent?"

Bridget promptly told the Inspector, "It was when the bell went for home time which was 4.30pm, I never saw him again after that." "Did you get on with Mr Dent?"

Bridget looked surprised the Inspector asked that question. "To be honest, I didn't like him at all."

"Why would that be Miss Molt?"

"Well Mr Dent wasn't a very nice man at all, he was

nothing but a bully and a woman molester." Bridget knew she had said too much.

The Inspector was a bit surprised she had said the last bit, so decided to push for more information. "What do you mean Mr Dent was a woman molester?"

"Well... everyone knew he was always hitting on the women in the factory."

"You sure you don't know who that could be, Miss Molt?"

"No, no one that I can think of, just what you hear around the factory."

"Lastly, Miss Molt, where were you between the hours of 10pm and 2.30am this morning?"

"Well, I was at the cinema with my friends Sylvia and Johnny. The film - Above and Beyond - finished at 10pm. We got some fish and chips, then we walked home."

"Right Miss Molt, I think that will be all for now."

FLASHBACK

The thing was, Bridget never forgot what Brian did to her. It all started well over a year ago when Bridget started working at All Parts. She prepared the wages each week and was really enjoying her job. Then one day Brian asked Bridget out on a date. She was shocked that he had asked her out as Brian was in his forties. She told him that she doesn't date people she works with because she didn't want to offend him and hoped that would be it.

Everything was fine for a short while, then one day

Brian checked the wages and said the wages for each person didn't add up. So, Brian accused Bridget of taking money off each worker and putting their wages lower than they should be. When Brian told her, Bridget went straight to the Manager's office crying which took Brian by surprise.

When the manager heard this, he had a feeling Brian was up to his old tricks. If he wasn't his brother-in-law, he would have sacked him ages ago. So, the manager told Bridget there had been a mistake and gave her a bonus to say sorry. It was clear to Bridget that Brian only accused her because she turned him down.

The Inspector looked on the list to see who was next to be questioned. "I see it is a Mr Hill. Let's see what he thinks of Mr Dent." As soon as PC Lamb brought Mr Johnny Hill in to be questioned, the Inspector asked him to take a seat. "In your own time, when was the last time you saw Mr Dent?"

Johnny first lit a cigarette before he answered the Inspector. Taking a puff of his cigarette, Johnny said, "It must have been yesterday when the bell went for home time, which was 4.30pm. Anyhow, how did Brian die?"

The Inspector studied Mr Hill for a moment, then said, "It is too early to say how Mr Dent died. Not until there has been a full post-mortem." The Inspector then asked, "Do you know of anyone who would harm Mr Dent?"

Johnny thought for a moment. "Most folk didn't like him. He was a nasty piece of work if you ask me."

"Also, could you tell me where you were between the hours of 10pm and 2:30am this morning?"

Johnny took another drag of his cigarette then spoke, "Well, from 10pm I was at the cinema with Sylvia Weston and Bridget Molt. We then got some fish and chips, then walked home to our beds."

"I think that will be all for now Mr Hill. We will call if we need to talk to you again." On that note the Inspector turned to PC Lamb, "We will have a break then ask the next one in."

As Johnny had been helping Sid sell the spare car parts down London. Brian had confronted Johnny the day before he was murdered, about his part in selling the spare parts. As with Sid Holmes, Brian threatened Johnny with the sack or going to prison for his part in the operation. So, Brian may have been getting money off Sid and Johnny.

Miss Vera Jones was the next to be questioned in the office. PC Lamb lead Miss Jones into the office. "Please take a seat, Miss Jones. In your own time could you tell me the last time you saw Mr Dent?"

"Let me see, it must have been when the bell went for home time. He asked me to type up some paperwork first thing the following morning."

"Would you say that was normal for Mr Dent to say to you?"

"Not really, you see there had been a mix up with an order a few days before. That is why Mr Dent asked Sylvia, Miss Weston, to sort out the files. He blamed her for the mix up. But, Inspector, Sylvia always keeps the files in order. I believe he made the mistake and to save his own skin he blamed her."

"I see, Miss Jones, thank you for clearing that up. So,

you say you didn't see Mr Dent after the bell went for home time?"

"Yes, that is what I am saying Inspector."

"Before you go, where were you between the hours of 10pm and 2.30am this morning?"

"You don't think I had anything to do with his murder, do you?"

"We've asked everyone who worked closely with Mr Dent, it's just a formality, Miss Jones."

"Well, I was at home all evening, then I went to bed around 10.30pm."

"Thank you, if we need anything else, we will be in touch."

The next on the list to be interviewed was Ken. Once PC Lamb called for Mr Ken Rollings, the Inspector then asked, "In your own time Mr Rollings, could you tell me when was the last time that you saw Mr Dent?"

Ken thought for a moment then told the Inspector, "It was yesterday when the bell went for home time, at 4.30pm."

"Yes, I see Mr Rollings. Do you know anyone who wished Mr Dent any harm?"

Ken went quiet for a brief moment then said, "Well, I understand many workers didn't like Mr Dent, as he could be hard to work with."

The inspector paused then asked, "So did you find Mr Dent hard to work with?"

"Not really as I usually just got on with my work. It was mostly the ladies who found him, let's say impossible to work with."

"Right, Mr Rollings. Lastly, could you tell me what you were doing from 10pm to 2.30am this morning?"

"I was at home reading the newspaper, then me and my wife Jenny went to bed, around 10.30pm." Right, Mr Rollings, I think that will be all for now. We will call for you if we need to speak with you again."

CHAPTER EIGHT

As soon as the bell went for lunch break, everyone made their way to the canteen. The talk of the day was Mr Dent. On Annie's table sat Sid, Henry, Wilma, Mable, Frank, Gilbert and Alfie. Even though no one liked Mr Dent, everyone was shocked to hear of his death.

"I know no one cared for Brian, but murder? That's another level!" Alfie said whilst taking a bite out of his sandwich. Annie and Wilma agreed with Alfie.

Annie went on to say, "It could be anyone from here. Not naming anyone, but even his own brother-in-law couldn't stand him. I heard that Mr Mortimer was fed up with him, always at his house complaining about everyone. He only put up with him because he was family." Annie, continued to say that "Brian, borrowed a lot of money as he was a gambler. That's what I heard anyway." she shrugged and carried on eating her lunch.

"I wonder if Mr Mortimer told the police all that?" Wilma said whilst stirring her cup of tea.

Sid went on to say, "I did hear that Brian was

hanging around the factory late last night. That is why Bill the caretaker found him in Mr Mortimer's office. Probably searching for something."

Annie then remembered something else about Brian. "Oh yes, I forgot there was something else. Johnny Hill told me a while back that Brian took a few bets off the workers. to make a bit of extra cash. Whoever killed him did them a favor. I hear the police are interviewing everyone who worked closely with him. So that means they won't bother us girls then."

"Yes, they will Annie, as you're the team leader, you collect the slips at the end of the day. Then take them to the wage's office," Sid reminded her.

Annie thought for a moment, "Oh yes I see what you mean, Sid. Never mind - I've got nothing to hide." Just after the bell went everyone in the canteen made their way back to work.

CHAPTER NINE

In the office, Sylvia was feeling anxious as she was the next one the police were to interview.

While sipping his coffee the Inspector sat down in front of the desk, waiting for Miss Weston to come in.

When PC Lamb called for Miss Weston to be questioned, Sylvia could feel all the other workers in the other offices looking at her. Maybe they knew Brian had made advances towards her. No, Sylvia knew Bridget and Johnny would not have told anyone about what Brian had done to her; they were two of her closest friends.

Sylvia made her way to the office, two doors down the corridor. She knew she had to tell them the truth about what Brian had done to her the day before.

Sitting in front of the Inspector, Sylvia could feel her face go crimson red, but she tried to keep cool.

"Could you tell me, Miss Weston, when was the last time you saw Mr Dent?" The Inspector could see Sylvia was nervous, so he added, "In your own time."

"Well, it all started six months ago, when I noticed Brian, I mean Mr Dent looking at me more than usual. At first, I thought nothing of it, I tried to ignore him looking at me but to be honest it made Mr. Dent do it even more. Then he started to make my tea at break time, which we usually take in turns to do."

"Mr Dent made it obvious he was sweet on me. It went on for weeks, it made me feel uncomfortable. As the others teased me. I know they didn't mean any harm, but deep down it was starting to make me feel bad. I can take a joke, but it was no joke to me."

"Then, one day, Mr Dent seemed to get the message and things went back to normal. Then around a month ago Mr. Dent asked me if I didn't mind staying behind an extra hour to sort out some paperwork for him. So, I said yes as I could do with the extra money. When I was nearly finished, Mr. Dent asked if I would like a cup of tea, so naturally I said yes!"

"Just as I finished my cup of tea, Mr Dent suddenly told me that he liked me and asked if I go out on a date with him. At first, I was shocked and felt awkward, so I told Mr Dent nicely, that I didn't really want to date anyone at the moment; and that I don't usually date anyone who I work with. It is easier that way, besides, I didn't like Mr Dent."

"At first Mr Dent would leave me alone, unless he needed me to do some work. Then a few weeks ago, Mr Dent, started making things hard for me."

"What do you mean, hard for you?" the Inspector asked.

"Well, like he would give me extra work to do, then

start moaning even if I was a minute late, that sort of thing. This went on right up until yesterday, when Mr. Dent... took it to the next level."

"Yesterday after work, Mr Dent asked me to sort out the filing cabinet. He said it was a right mess, even though I didn't do it. So, I stayed behind. But just as I was about to leave the office, Mr Dent suddenly grabbed me hard. He then slowly moved his hand onto my crotch! I pushed him away, grabbed my bag then ran out of the office."

"When I was outside, I felt so degraded like it was me who encouraged him, but - believe me Inspector - I didn't. I just wanted him to stop. I went straight to the café around the corner, where my friend Bridget was waiting for me. That was the last time I spoke to and saw Mr. Dent."

"Thank you, Miss Weston, I know that must have been hard for you to tell me. Lastly Miss Weston, where were you between the hours of 10pm and 2.30am?"

Sylvia thought for a moment then answered "I was at the cinema with my friends Bridget Molt and Johnny Hill. After the film finished, we walked home."

"I think that will be all for now, we will be in touch if we need you any further."

As soon as Sylvia left the room, she was feeling so relieved that she had been honest with the Inspector. The Inspector had all he needed from the workers in Mr Dent's office, for now anyway.

CHAPTER TEN

By the time Sylvia got back to her desk, it was nearly time for home. Johnny and Bridget could not wait to ask Sylvia how it went with the Inspector. "I was so glad I was honest and got things off my chest." Johnny and Bridget were so pleased that it was all over for Sylvia.

As she got to her desk, Johnny smiled and winked at her. She beamed while putting a sheet of paper in her typewriter.

Bridget quietly asked Sylvia and Johnny if they were coming to the dance at the Crystal Rooms which were on every Friday and Saturday night. "Yes, I will be coming." Sylvia whispered. Johnny put his thumb up.

As soon as the bell went for home time, everyone was more than ready to leave with it being a Friday and pay day.

"You two ladies coming for a coffee, my treat?" Johnny asked Sylvia.

"Why not," she said.

"Where's Bridget?" Johnny asked.

"She has just nipped to the loo," Sylvia smiled.

"I will go and get the drinks in then." Johnny went on to the café.

As Bridget came out of the toilets, she could hear someone talking. In fact, it was the Inspector talking to PC Lamb. "I think we will wait for the post-mortem tomorrow, then re-interview the office workers. Someone must have seen something."

Bridget, then waited until the Inspector and PC Lamb had gone before she left. When Bridget got to the café, Johnny and Sylvia were already sat waiting for her. "You will never guess what I overheard when I was in the loo?"

After Bridget told them what she overheard, Sylvia said, "The police must not have much to go on if they want to interview everyone again."

"Whoever it was who killed Brian, did everyone a favor." Bridget went on as she lit a cigarette. "Anyhow, we will have a good time at the Crystal Rooms tonight."

"Yes, we will have some fun tonight." Sylvia said while sipping her coffee.

By now, the café was starting to get crowded. Most of the factory workers ended up in the café, on a Friday. "Hey Sid?" Johnny shouted. "Are you and the missus coming to the Crystal Rooms, tonight?" Sid could not hear Johnny very well as the juke box was playing music.

He came over to where Johnny was sitting with Sylvia and Bridget. "We may be going to the Crystal Rooms, depends on if we can get a babysitter for the kids. Suzie's Mum usually has them, but if we can we'll see you up there." Sid looked uncomfortable, then quizzed Johnny on if he knew anything about Brian's death.

"All I know, Sid, is Brian was found dead in the manager's office. No one can understand why he was in there."

"He was probably nosing about as usual," Sid went on to say.

"I suppose the police will find out soon enough." Johnny said.

"I better be off, else my tea be in the dog?" Sid joked, then left the café.

After a short while, Sylvia, Bridget and Johnny left to catch the bus home.

CHAPTER ELEVEN

With it being a Friday night most of the factory workers went up to the Crystal Rooms. It was a place where folk could have a dance, drink and let their hair down. By 9 o'clock it was starting to get busy, playing everyone's favourite songs.

Annie, Wilma and Mable had just gotten their drinks from the bar when they saw there were empty seats going by the entrance. After settling down, Annie said. "I wonder if Frank will be coming tonight?" Frank was one of the machinists at All Parts. He was a strong bloke who did boxing tall, dark and handsome. Annie had liked Frank for a while now.

"Look Mable, Annie has got her eye on Frank."

"So, what if I do? Frank is single, I found out today."

"Who told you he was single?" Mable wondered.

"It was Gilbert Minton, who told me. He should know, they're best friends, in fact."

"I just wondered Annie, don't get your knickers in a

twist." After their discussion all three girls started to laugh. By now they were quite tipsy, from the Gin and Tonic they had been drinking.

It was not long until Frank, Henry and Gilbert were also at the dance. Wilma and Mable secretly liked Gilbert and Henry, as they were also single. Gilbert and Henry also did boxing and all the girls in the factory thought they were fit too. The group of girls watched as the three men headed straight to the bar.

After a few more drinks Annie, Wilma and Mable were enjoying the music and got up to dance. Even though Annie liked Frank, she knew not to run after him. Her dad would always tell her, "Lass, always let the man do the chasing." She knew it was the right thing to do. Even Wilma and Mable thought the same as Annie and all three girls were more than happy just to dance for now.

All night Frank, Gilbert and Henry, were watching the girls dance from the bar. Not long after 10:30, Annie noticed some Soldiers come in. The Soldiers went straight to the bar, ordered a drink then, out of the blue, they went over to the girls. They asked Annie, Wilma and Mable for a dance and, without hesitation, the girls said yes. The whole time Frank, Gilbert and Henry watched from the bar.

CHAPTER TWELVE

After going to a few local pubs, Johnny, Sylvia and Bridget made their way to the Crystal Rooms. When they got there, it was quite busy. With it so crowded it took a while for Johnny to order the drinks, after turning too quickly and nearly spilling them down himself, Johnny eventually made his way to where Sylvia and Bridget were sat.

Despite everything that had happened that day, the three of them were in good spirits and keen to start dancing and the music was only making them want to get on the dance floor more. It was not long until Sylvia noticed Frank at the bar. You see, she had liked him for a while now and he was looking straight over to where Sylvia was dancing.

"I can see him looking over at you, Sylvia. I reckon you have a good chance at getting with him tonight."

"Do you think so?" Sylvia hoped she did have a chance of getting with Frank, but Wilma had told her a few days ago that Annie liked him as well.

While Johnny stood by the bar, he could see Sid and his wife Suzi sitting in the corner of the room. Johnny thought he would go over but, when he got closer, he could see them arguing. So, before they noticed, he turned and went back over to the bar instead. Johnny thought it was strange that Sid and Suzi were arguing, they usually got on fine.

It wasn't long before Gilbert got talking about the murder. "So, what you think about Brian Dent?" Gilbert asked curiously.

"News has it that Brian was stabbed in the heart, while he was working." Henry went on to say.

"That is news to me." Gilbert replied. Johnny looked surprised at the fact that Henry knew how he was killed.

"Well one of the Police Officers is friends with my neighbour," Henry went on to say, before taking a sip of his pint.

Johnny chose this moment to get involved in the conversation, "I hear the police are interviewing everyone at the station from Monday." Henry quizzed Johnny on how he had come to hear that. "Well, Bridget overheard the Inspector tell a PC outside the back entrance of the factory earlier today."

"That won't go down too well with the management: they won't want all the workers going to the police station," Johnny said before ordering another pint.

After Johnny got his pint of lager, he looked to see if Sid and Suzi were still arguing but, when Johnny looked over to where they were sitting, they had gone.

CHAPTER THIRTEEN

After the weekend, everyone felt refreshed ready to be back at work. It was raining and would be for the rest of the day, so when the Inspector and PC Green showed up it just added to the misery.

As the Inspector stood where the body was found a thought came to him, whoever murdered Mr. Dent, it looked like a planned kill. With a rubber glove found at the scene. The force of the knife wound suggests it may have been a male who committed the murder.

"Shall I call for the first one, Gov?" PC Green asked the Inspector.

"Yes please," the Inspector said, lost in his trail of thoughts.

The Inspector had now decided to interview the rest of the workers at the factory. First it was Mr. Sid Holmes to be questioned, as he had contact with Mr. Dent. As soon as Mr. Holmes entered the office, he took a seat. By now Sid was starting to feel anxious as to what the Inspector was going to ask him.

"Could you tell me, Mr Holmes, when was the last time you saw Mr Dent"?

Sid thought for a minute then told the Inspector, "It must have been around 5.30pm on Thursday when I took Mr Dent the daily slips to his office."

"Would you say exactly 5.30pm or around then?" The Inspector waited for a reply.

"It was just after, as I was on the factory floor. I glanced at the clock, and it said 5.30pm. I went to put some rat poison down straight after as there has been quite a few rats on the factory floor. You see the women scream when they see one and cause a panic. With it being poison you need gloves on.

"Yes, I can see that, Mr Holmes. Do you often put poison down?"

"Yes, I do mostly in the winter months, when the rats come in rummaging for food left by the workers. It's usually me or David Jenson, the other supervisor. But it was my turn last Thursday. Well, Inspector, the trouble is, soon as you put the poison down, the buggers are back again, pardon my language."

"Just one more question Mr Holmes, where were you from 10pm to the early hours of Friday 4th of April… say 2.30am?"

Sid thought for a moment. "Well, I went for a few pints in my local pub - the Hen and Chickens - 'til around 10.30pm, then went home to bed. My misses was asleep, if I remember."

"Thank you, Mr Holmes. I think that will be all for now." The Inspector gave a slight smile as he watched Mr Holmes leave.

PC Green then sent for the next worker to be questioned, Mr Henry Davidson. Henry was a fit lad who worked hard for his pay. As soon as Henry got to the office to be questioned the Inspector asked Mr. Davidson to take a seat, just like the other workers.

The Inspector asked, "In your own time, could you tell me the last time you had seen or spoken with Mr Dent?"

"What I can remember is that I finished packing just before the bell had gone for home time which was 4.30pm. I was quite happy with myself, as I packed an extra twenty parts, with it being on piece work, every extra money comes in handy. I then took my slip to Sid, our supervisor, but he wasn't around so I went up to the office. Again, there was no one about, so I left mine on Mr Holmes' desk."

"So, you are saying you never see Mr Dent after you finished for the day?" Inspector Wright was trying hard to understand what Mr Davidson was saying. "So, when was the last time you saw Mr Dent that day?"

"It must have been in the day I saw Mr Dent. He was talking with Johnny Hill outside the back of the factory as I went out on my afternoon break. Mr Dent was sort of arguing with Johnny about something. They were too far away for me to hear what was being said."

The Inspector was quite interested in what Henry had just said, so he pushed him for more information. "So, was that the last time you saw Mr Dent that day?"

"Yes, that is what I am saying."

"Just one more thing, what did you think of Mr Dent?"

"I never had much to do with Mr Dent really. Most folk around here didn't think much about him."

"Lastly, Mr. Davidson where were you on the 3rd. of April and the 4th of April, between 10pm and 2.30am in the morning?"

"Well, I was Boxing till 9.30pm then I went to the pub called the Falling Star with Frank Cane and Gilbert Minton. We were there till about 10.45pm then we went home."

"Thank you, Mr Davidson. I think that will be all for now."

Just as the Inspector was going to interview Mr Frank Cane, PC Lamb came into the office. "The results of the post-mortem have just come in, Gov." PC Lamb told the Inspector that Mr Dent had died of a single knife wound to the heart. Possibly a pocketknife. The killer most certainly was right-handed. Which he would have died instantly. The killer must have killed Mr Dent with great force.

There were also low doses of Thallium found in his body. He may not even had any symptoms. Thallium is mostly found in rat poison. Was the killer trying to poison Mr Dent first or was it that the rat poison wasn't working fast enough so the killer stabbed him instead? So many possibilities.

Later that day the Inspector decided to go and take another look at Mr Dent's lodgings and to speak with his land lady. The Inspector said to PC Lamb that he would finish interviewing the workers the following day.

Once Inspector Wright and PC Lamb reached Mr Dent's lodgings, 33 Pond Road, the Inspector knocked on the door. A frail, grey-haired lady slowly opened the door. Her name was Mrs Ruby Reynolds a sharp mouthed lady. "What do you want this time?" Mrs Reynolds demanded.

"We need to look over Mr Dent's room again, we have a search warrant," the Inspector said as he stood waving it in Mrs Reynolds' face. "We have the right to search Mr Dent's room at any time," the Inspector hoped this would keep Mrs Reynolds quiet.

Mrs Reynolds stood in the doorway a while, just to make a point, but eventually she gave in with a smirk on her face. She then tried to come up with the Inspector and PC Lamb, but PC Lamb said, "We have got it from here." Mrs Reynolds stood there for a moment, then PC Lamb told her to go for the second time. Eventually she left.

This time, the Inspector wanted to search Mr Dent's lodgings himself. The Inspector had a gut feeling there must be something in Mr Dent's room that could help him with this case. Mr. Dents room was quite plain really, with just a single bed, one small table and chair and shabby green curtains hanging over a small window. As the Inspector stood in the doorway looking in the room, something made him look at the floor. It wasn't long until the Inspector noticed something looked out of place. The floor was uneven. The Inspector put his hand in his pocket and pulled out his pocketknife. He then bent down, so he could pull a small piece of the floorboard up as it was loose.

Once the board had been removed the Inspector reached below the floorboards and pulled out a small note pad and money rolled up with an elastic band. The note pad had a list of names written inside that looked very familiar to the Inspector. Why would a supervisor in a factory have a note pad and rolled up money hidden away in the floorboards of his digs? The Inspector had a feeling it may be, black mail.

After putting the floorboard back down again, the Inspector looked at the note pad to see what the secret was for hiding it under the floorboards. There was a small list of names of workers from the factory with prices next to the names. The Inspector thought he would look at it closer at the police station.

CHAPTER FOURTEEN

As soon as the Inspector and PC Lamb returned to the police station, the Inspector sat at his desk. There, he got the writing pad out to take a closer look to see what Mr Dent had written. With the names, the Inspector started to realise why so many of the factory workers hated him.

The Inspector honestly could not believe there was such a person who could do this to all these people. Mr Dent, you see, was not just black mailing one person, but at least four people and most likely more. Their names could not stand out any bigger.

But there was just one snag, it did not say what he was black mailing them for - just how much he collected from them each week. The Inspector had a good idea that the killer could well be on this list. There was one thing about the Inspector when he lived and worked in London, he was known for catching his killer. That is one reason Manchester police wanted him to work with them.

The first person on the list was Mr Sid Holmes, the

floor supervisor. Miss Annie Bright, Mr Roger Mortimer, the Manager, and Mr Johnny Hill. Some of them had a question mark by their names, could mean Brian wasn't sure whether to black mail them or not. The trouble is, will they come clean to what Mr. Dent was black mailing them for? They'll have to because just having names in a writing pad will not stand up in court.

Wasting no time, the Inspector asked PC Lamb and PC Green to accompany him back to the factory.

When the Inspector and PCs reached the factory, they made their way to the office where they were doing their questioning. The Inspector asked PC Green to bring Mr Frank Cane in first. He was being questioned because he was a team leader in charge and sometimes took the slips to Brian's office. "Please Mr Cane, could you tell me when the last time you saw or spoke to Mr Dent?" The Inspector gave a lingering stare, waiting patiently for an answer.

"I would say it was before the bell went for home time. I remember distantly as I was in a good mood because I did more parts that day. So, before I went home, I took the slips straight to the office because I couldn't find Sid Holmes. I never saw him again, as the next day he was found dead."

"I see Mr Cane, what did you think of Mr Dent as a person?"

Frank went quiet for a moment, then said, "To be honest I don't know him personally, but I hear he wasn't a nice man."

"Last of all, Mr Cane, where were you on the night of Mr Dent's murder?" The Inspector waited for an answer, curious as to whether his alibi be the same as Mr Davidson's.

"That night I was boxing till around 9.30pm, then me, Henry and Gilbert went for a couple of drinks in the Falling Star. I think we all left the same time about 10.30pm, then we went home."

"Well, I think that will be all for now, Mr Cane. You can go now."

FLASH BACK

As Frank left the office, there was just one thing he did not tell the Inspector.

Many years ago Frank's Dad worked for All Parts long before Frank was working there. His dad had worked in the office doing the wage slips. Mr. Cane Senior had worked there for many years, he hoped to retire there and collect his pension.

A young Brian Dent worked there then; he hadn't been supervisor for long, just six months. Being the supervisor, supposed it went to his head. Brian didn't like Mr Cane Senior, as in everyone's eyes he could do no wrong. When Brian accused him of tampering with the wage slips, making out the workers had less money which Mr Cane Senior never did. He was a trusting fellow and Brian made out he was a criminal.

Brian made it look like Mr Cane senior cashed in on the money that he'd stolen from the other workers and took it up with management. Of course, there was no evidence that Mr Cane Senior had even taken the money, so management said they would press no charges, but fired him anyway. Unfortunately, before he could collect his pension.

Mr Cane Senior was not the same after that, in fact he suffered a heart attack from all the stress losing his job caused and turned him into an old man overnight. Now, every day, all that Mr. Cane Senior does is sit in his armchair waiting for his son Frank to come home and tell him how his day went at All Parts.

The Inspector could see it wasn't going to be an easy case this time. He knew he would have to play his tactics different this time. The Inspector thought whoever he asked on the list, would keep their story. They were scared that they would be arrested for Mr Dent's murder.

However, there is one thing Inspector Wright had learned, there is always one that will crack in time. That one person may be the key to cracking the case. Even if they hadn't murdered anyone. With the murder scene being at a factory, the Inspector realised it would be harder to question all the workers so decided only to question those who had close contact with Mr. Dent.

As Annie Bright was a packer, and the team leader, she would have taken the slips to the office. The Inspector asked PC Green to call her in next.

When Annie got to the office, she was asked to take a seat.

"Could you tell me the last time you saw or spoke to Mr. Dent?"

"It was when I took the slips to the office at the end of the day, which was 4.30pm. Mr. Dent wasn't there so I left them on his desk. I did see the other workers in the office though. It must have been the day before when I last saw Mr. Dent. Which would have been Wednesday around 4.30pm."

"Now could you tell me where were you between 10pm and 2.30am the following morning"" I was in my flat all evening, then went to bed at 10.15pm." The Inspector knows that everyone he interviews will say they were in bed around 2.30am. But one of them won't be. "Thank you, Miss Bright you can go. If I need to speak with you again, we will let you know."

The Inspector could see no one will say they were being black mailed by Mr Dent. They were all saying the same thing. Like the rest of the workers, he let Miss Bright go back to her work.

CHAPTER FIFTEEN

FLASH BACK

Annie was feeling nervous as she had a secret, she did not want anyone knowing. It all started around a year ago. How Brian Dent found out was a mystery to Annie. Well Annie was not particularly good with her money she would buy things like clothes, shoes, bags that sort of thing. To be honest it became an obsession and got that bad she never had the money to pay her bills.

Annie was a foot loose and fancy free 22-year-old who lived in a small flat on the outskirts of Manchester. It was only right that she liked to look good when she went on nights out.

On one of Annie's nights out, she went in a bar where Lawyers, Doctors and Politicians would hang out. This One particular night, Annie was beside herself as she owed a lot of money. Her spending was out of control. As Annie sipped her drink, this pretty girl came over and sat on a seat next to her. After a while Annie and this girl started talking, they were getting on well. They then started talking about their lives.

Feeling comfortable with this girl, who had introduced herself as Betsy, Annie began telling her about her spending and that she needed to find money fast to pay for her bills. To Annie's surprise Betsy went on to tell her all about her job. How she makes loads of money. Betsy then said she could get Annie a job where she works.

Annie, feeling intrigued with it all, wanted to know more. "All you have to do is to dress up really smart and go on dates with these Gentlemen?" At this point Annie should have run but being naive, she thought this was her way out of debt. Betsy eagerly told Annie she would get all these lovely clothes to wear, and that she was pretty and had a good figure. Betsy told Annie she would get a job easy, all she had to do is show up for an interview. Annie agreed to go for an interview.

Betsy told Annie, "I will go and make a call to my boss." After Betsy had been gone a while, she eventually returned to tell Annie to go to an address that she'd scribbled on a piece of paper the next morning at 10.30am.

Annie was really pleased she had the chance to earn good money and that all her problems would be over. She did not really know what she was getting herself into but thanked Betsy for helping her anyway. Betsy smiled, "No problem, we will see each other again soon."

By the next morning, Annie was feeling nervous and excited about the possibility of earning extra money.

When Annie got to the address for her interview, she was surprised it was at a house. Feeling nervous, As Annie knocked on the door, she felt the first doubt creep into her mind. Just as she was about to leave, someone opened the door.

It was a lady dressed smartly with a lot of makeup on and shoulder length blonde hair. Annie started to wonder if she was in the right place, then the lady spoke in a soft voice.

"Hello, you must be Annie, I am Gladys. Come in my dear." Annie was surprised the lady was so friendly.

As she nervously entered the house, Gladys offered her a seat. The room was very tidy, with leopard skin cushions on a black leather sofa. The black- and gold-colored curtains were closed with two large lamps on each side of the room. Gladys offered Annie a drink, but she shook her head and politely declined.

"Well shall we get down to business? I guess Betsy has filled you in on how we do things around here. Well Annie, let's see you" Annie not sure what she should do asked Gladys what she wanted her to do. Gladys smiled, "Mind my manners, I want you to stand up my dear."

Annie slowly stood up, wondering why Gladys wanted her to do so. "You are a pretty girl, Annie. With a little help you will do perfectly. You can sit down now." Gladys ordered in a low voice. "This is how it works Annie. You dress in fine clothes, which I provide for you, put some make up on - which you don't need much of. Maybe have your hair pinned up. Then our clients ask me to provide a girl to go on a date with them that they previously chosen. Is this something you may be interested in?"

Annie looked at Gladys and spoke. "Yes, I think so. If you think I am suitable." All Annie was thinking about was to get out of the debt she was in.

Gladys laughed and spoke, "Yes, you are suitable, my dear." Annie realised she had forgotten to ask how much the pay was. After Gladys told her how much she would be earning, just for one date. Annie was more than happy to work for Gladys. "So, if you could return here around 5.30pm this evening we can get you dressed and have your make-up done ready for a date. Do you have a day job?" Annie nodded. "I think that is everything. See you at 5.30pm then Annie." As Annie had rung in sick from work, she made her way home.

That was over a year ago. Annie knew deep down that it was seedy, but she was desperate for some money. The first date Annie had was with a businessman in his forties that she'd met in the same bar she had met Betsy.

After Annie met the client, he took her to a hotel outside Manchester. She had hated every minute, the client was understanding, but it did not help her. When Annie got home, she cried all night. Eventually it did get better as the weeks went by, but Annie regretted ever going to that house that day.

So that is why she never wanted her family and friends ever knowing she worked as an escort. Brian found out about three months ago. You see when Annie was working as an escort, she was to meet a gentleman in this restaurant. Annie not knowing that Brian used that particular restaurant. Wasn't long till Brian worked out, what Annie was doing on her evenings off. He said, "I know you're an escort, a posh word for a wore if you ask me. "I will tell your family and friends, you get the picture?" Brian knew Annie was earning good money at the escort place. So, he thought he would take his cut. So that is why Annie didn't want the Inspector knowing what she was doing for Brian to black mail her.

Mr Mortimer, the Manager was next on the list, so the Inspector decided to question him again. PC Lamb asked Mr Mortimer to come in the empty office next to his.

"Thank you, Mr. Mortimer," the Inspector began, "I just want to ask you a few questions. In your own time could you tell me, why do you think Mr Dent was in your office late on the 4th of April?"

Mr Mortimer looked nervous as a small, but obvious, bead of sweat ran down his forehead "I can't really say for sure why Mr. Dent was in my office on the night he was killed. As I mentioned, he had a key to my office in case I was away".

The Inspector took a long look at Mr Mortimer, then went on to say. "I believe Mr Dent was in your office trying to get information about you. What do you say to that, Mr Mortimer?"

By now Mr Mortimer was sweating excessively, and he had gone red in the face. Eventually he told the Inspector. "I didn't kill Brian I swear I didn't."

"I see Mr Mortimer; then would you have killed Mr Dent if he was blackmailing you? Inspector Wright waited for an answer.

Mr Mortimer looked down his face full of shame

then told the Inspector "No I was not being blackmailed"

He still chose to keep his secret from the Inspector. Even though the Inspector knew he was being blackmailed by Brian Dent.

You see, the real reason Mr Mortimer had been hiding, was the fact he used to have escort girls up in his office late at night. Away from his wife. As he didn't want her finding out. Mr. Mortimer had been having escort girls up in his office for months. That is how Brian had found out, about them. A while back Brian had left some paperwork in his office earlier that day. So later that night he went to pick the papers up from his office. As Brian passed, Mr Mortimer's office, he saw him laughing and messing around, half naked with this escort girl, drinking wine. Mr Mortimer never knew Brian had saw him that night. Not till Brian started to black mail him.

CHAPTER SIXTEEN

When Johnny went to be questioned by the Inspector again, Sylvia and Bridget wondered if they would be called in again.

"Johnny has been gone for a while now," Bridget whispered to Sylvia, while they were making up the wage slips for Friday.

"I know. I do hope everything is alright?" Sylvia was concerned.

Vera, the eldest lady in the office, was busy with the orders coming in. Usually, Vera would keep her head down and get on with her jobs, but today she was more talkative and asking all kinds of questions. In a way Vera was lucky as Brian had never bothered her.

Not long after, Johnny returned, Sylvia and Bridget were eager to know what the police had asked him. "Just the same old questions, waste of time if you ask me," he told them with a cheeky grin.

After Vera talked to Sylvia and Bridget about the works picnic on the Saturday. Hoping the weather was going to be good. Vera went over to ask Johnny if she could talk with him after work. "I'm all yours Vera," Johnny said and gave her a friendly wink.

No sooner had the bell gone for home time, everyone had left their places and headed to clock out for the day. Before Sylvia and Bridget clocked out, they both finished their work they were doing. Sylvia shouted over to Johnny that she and Bridget would meet him in the café. Johnny cheerfully said, "I will meet you two after I have spoken to Vera."

While Sylvia and Bridget were in the café waiting for Johnny, Sylvia put a song on the jukebox. *When I Fall in Love* by Doris Day. "I should have known you would put this song on," Bridget laughed as she sipped her coffee.

"I love this song, what's your problem?" Sylvia sarcastically said walking back to her seat. Just as she sat down, Johnny waltzed in.

"I've just ordered you a coffee!" Bridget shouted to Johnny. After Johnny paid for his coffee, he went to sit by Sylvia and Bridget. "What did Vera want with you Johnny?" Sylvia questioned.

"Oh, it was just some paperwork she found in Brian's desk, nothing to worry about," Johnny said as he lit a cigarette.

"Just two days now 'till we go on the picnic." Bridget changed the subject as soon as it was clear there was nothing more interesting to Johnny's chat with Vera. The union organises a picnic every month during spring and summer. Each person had to take something that is sorted out between all of the workers so that nobody doubles up and they end up with thirty cheese sandwiches and no drinks.

"I wonder who will be going?" Sylvia wondered, while taking a drag of her cigarette.

"Forecast says it will be warm and sunny this Saturday."

"With the fair and band on, it should be a good day out." Bridget always looked forward to going to the picnic. "Don't forget to take your radio!" Bridget reminded Sylvia.

"No, I won't," Sylvia said trying to be happy about it - she was never as excited as Bridget when it came to the picnic.

"Cheer up, we will have fun, you'll see."

"As long as it isn't raining," Sylvia hit back, being as hopeful as she could.

"My aunt always says 'you got to make your own fun," Bridget tells Sylvia. By now the café was getting busy, with quite a few from the factory that usually came in to unwind once they'd finished work.

"Man United play Liverpool on Saturday. Should be a good game," Johnny said to Sylvia and Bridget. Then he noticed Sid on one of the games on the other side of the café. "Give me a minute, ladies," he said, stamping out his cigarette and heading over to Sid.

"Are you up for going to The Running Hare on Saturday? Man, United play Liverpool - it'll be a good game."

"Yeah, I'm up for it. I am taking Suzi and the kids to the picnic first. Gilbert, Frank and Henry will also be going, to the picnic" Sid says to Johnny.

"That will be great. I'll get a crate of beer to take to the picnic." Sid asks Johnny where he is getting the beer from. "I got a mate who works at The Running Hare he owes me a favor or two."

"All right then, mate. Will see you on Saturday," Sid said before he left the café.

CHAPTER SEVENTEEN

By the time Saturday came, there was no more evidence in the case of Brian Dent and Inspector Wright was finding the case challenging.

There were many suspects being blackmailed and so many more who seemed to have their own reasons to hate the man. He was sure that one day someone would slip up and he would get his break, but it was a case of waiting.

There was something else bothering him: how did Brian Dent get Thallium in his body? There must be something the Inspector was overlooking somehow. The Inspector had taken all the case files home so he could go over the interviews with the workers. He wanted to check if he was missing anything. As it was a warm, sunny day the Inspector was sitting in his garden. Even though it was his day off, he still could not stop thinking about the case.

The Inspector had only been married to Penny for two years. The move from London to Manchester had been a challenge for them both and their small baby, Alice, hadn't made it any easier.

FLASHBACK

While the Inspector was going through the files, something made him think of a similar case in London. It was around two years ago now. The Inspector never found out who did that murder, as the case was left open.

A grocery store murder with the victim having been stabbed through the heart. The Inspector thought it very strange the two cases seemed so alike. Trying not to think too much into it, he decided to just interview the office workers again on the following Monday. He would make them know he'd only be questioning them. Perhaps that would shake them up a bit. One of them must know something and maybe he could get one of them to finally make a mistake.

While sitting in his garden, the Inspector had an idea to go to Heaton Park. He knew that All parts were having one of their monthly work picnics and he thought he could pop by to way things up a bit. So, when the Inspector's wife came outside to bring him a cup of tea, he asked her if she would like to go to the park as the fair would be there. He thought it be nice for his wife to get to meet some new people.

She thought it was a great idea. "I will go and make sandwiches and take some of the cupcakes I made this morning." The Inspector smiled as Penny rushed into the kitchen.

Once she had gotten all the food and drinks together, she went to get Alice from her crib. On their way to Heaton Park Penny says, "We are lucky the weather is good for the time of year, considering it's only April" After the Inspector had parked the car, he got Alice's push chair from the boot.-As before the three of them set off toward the large group of people that had gathered in the park. It wasn't until then that the Inspector started to wonder if it was a good idea to come.

As the Inspector and Penny walked through the park, they could hear the music from the fair. They strolled happily for a few minutes before they decided it would be nice to sit on the riverbank. While the Inspector dealt with Alice and Penny sorted the picnic out, a thought occurred to her.

"If I know you - and I do - I bet this as something to do with work"

"Darling, I thought as it's a lovely sunny day, we should make the most of it. And yes, it has got something to do with work… a bit." Penny tried to keep a straight face, but she and the Inspector laughed as it occurred to them both how transparent he was to his wife.

The Inspector was a fair man, he believed a man or woman was innocent until proven guilty. When he was a teenager living in London, he'd not had an easy life. His Parents lived on a rundown estate and there weren't many jobs, so his father took what he could get to keep food on the table. Most of the people who lived on the estate weren't the sort to mix with and the Inspector had hung around with the wrong crowd. They would break into houses on richer estates and steal anything of value to sell for money.

When One day while the gang was out burgling, one of the neighbours called the police. Most of the boys had gotten away, but the Inspector was caught and taken to the station.

As the Inspector was only fifteen at the time, he was sent to a juvenile facility. He vowed from that day that he would turn his life around. His Parents eventually moved from the estate and moved to a better location. When the Inspector had done his time in a juvenile facility he got a job working with his father delivering groceries. Then, later, the police. He worked his way up from nothing to being a successful, well-respected Inspector. So, for that reason, Inspector Wright knew everyone deserved a second chance.

CHAPTER EIGHTEEN

Sylvia was feeling happy about going to the picnic. She was in a much better mood than she had been a few days before.

She was on the lookout for Gregg, a fireman that she had met in the pub and had a soft spot for. She knew the fire service was going to be there at Heaton Park doing a demonstration for the kids.

Ever since she met him in The Old Slipper a few months ago, he had always spoken to her. He was tall, dark and handsome, and Sylvia had a true crush on him. With it being a lovely day, Sylvia thought the only thing to make the day perfect was if he was there.

After Sylvia got dressed, she made her way downstairs to the kitchen. While she was having some toast and a cup of tea, she remembered to take her new camera with her. She had only used it a few times since she had gotten it for her birthday off her Mum and Dad.

"Mum did you get the ham and bread I asked you to

get?" Sylvia shouted to her Mum as soon as she walked in from the shop.

"Yes, I have got everything you asked for. I even got some cakes from the bakery."

Sylvia gave her Mum a kiss on the cheek in approval. "Thanks Mum, I better get on and make the sandwiches. I think I will do cheese and ham, and just ham on its own." She also had crisps and chocolate bars to take with her.

It took about half an hour for Sylvia to make all the sandwiches and pack them into bags. After, Sylvia quickly ran upstairs to get a blanket and her camera. She was ready to go and meet Bridget at 12 o'clock.

Everyone would be taking their friends and family to Heaton Park but Sylvia's Mum and Dad had to go and visit her Nan in the hospital. Nothing serious, she'd had a fall a few weeks ago, but was on the mend now. That's why Sylvia didn't feel bad about not going with them.

Just before Sylvia was about to leave, there was a knock on the door. It was Bridget.

"Hi, I thought I was meeting you at the bus stop?" Sylvia looked surprised to see her friend standing there.

"I was ready early so I thought I would call for you instead. Everything all right with you?" Bridget asked.

"Yes, everything is fine with me, we better be off else we'll miss the bus." Sylvia put everything in a trolley, so it was easier to manage on the bus.

On the bus Sylvia asked Bridget what she was taking to the picnic.

"Well, my Mum baked cheese and ham quiches. I also brought pop and crisps."

"I will have some of the quiches, as I know your Mum is a good cook."

"I suppose you can have a small piece," Bridget teased and the pair started to laugh.

By the time Sylvia and Bridget got to the park it was quite busy - most of the workers were with their families. Sid was with his wife Suzi and their three kids. Alfie was also with his wife Wendy and two kids. Annie was with Wilma and Mable who had each brought their mums.

Everyone had put blankets down on the grass, so they could sit down. Not too far away the children were playing football or ball games. With the sun shining down, it looked like everyone was having fun.

A short time after, Frank, Henry and Gilbert arrived with Frank's kid brother George. George went over to the other kids who were playing football while the men walked over to where Annie was sat with Wilma, Mable and their families. "I see you three haven't brought anything," Annie gave Frank, Henry and Gilbert a lingering stare. Frank just laughed awkwardly.

CHAPTER NINETEEN

Once Sylvia and Bridget put the food with the rest, they debated on where they would sit. "I think we should sit on the riverbank and feed the ducks," Sylvia suggested as she looked around absentmindedly.

Bridget frowned, wondering why Sylvia would want to sit by the river with all the bugs around. "I thought we could watch the ducks as we sat near the river bank."

Sylvia could see Bridget wasn't happy sitting by the riverbank, so they looked for somewhere else to go. After putting the blanket down for the ninth time, both agreed to compromise and sit by an old oak tree instead. Sylvia then put the radio on, she thought it would cheer things up a bit.

Each of the workers' families put all the food together, so everyone could choose what they wanted to eat. Once all the food was in one place, it looked like it was going to feed the five thousand.

After a short while Johnny turned up and, as soon as he found where Sylvia and Bridget were sitting, he made his way over to them.

"I see you have brought something," Sylvia looked excitedly at what Johnny had in his hand.

"Oh, here you go, got a crate of beer from The Running Hare. "Got a mate who works there, he owes me a favour."

"Well at least you brought something! I hear Frank, Henry and Gilbert brought nowt."

"Well, there you go!" Johnny looked smug with himself. "Let's get this party started." Johnny gave Sylvia and Bridget a bottle of beer each.

"We are not at the Crystal Rooms you know," Sylvia joked, after she took a swig of her beer.

A short while after - Sylvia had already reached for a second bottle - Johnny noticed Sid with his family. "I won't be long, just going over to see Sid."

While Sid's wife and kids were playing ball games on the grass Johnny walked over to where Sid was standing. Lighting a cigarette Johnny asked Sid, "Hey mate, you got any parts for me to sell?"

"Well, Johnny, I thought we should keep a low profile for a while… Well, until the police stop coming to the factory."

Johnny was the one who would sell the parts on the black market down London. Nodding his head Johnny agreed with Sid.

They both joined in playing with the kids at football. Everyone was enjoying the day out with their friends and family. Not long after, everyone was starting to get hungry, so they went over to where the food was on the grass.

"It's a lovely spread, there's so much food to be eaten," Annie gushed unsure of what to pick first. By now the band had started playing, and on the other side of the park the fire brigade was showing the kids how things worked and letting them sit in the fire engine.

When Sylvia went to get some food, she noticed that Gregg was there with the fire brigade. He did not notice her. She was not sure whether or not to go and say hello she wanted to but wasn't sure what to say to him. Sylvia thought, *If only I had a few Gin and Tonics to have the courage to speak to him.* You see Bridget didn't know about Gregg; he was Sylvia's secret admirer.

When Sylvia went back to where she was sitting by the oak tree, she was debating whether or not she should tell Bridget about Gregg. Then Sylvia thought she would just come out and say it. "I've got something to tell you."

"Oh, what is it?"

"Well, a few months ago I got talking to this bloke, a fireman. Well, he is here, showing the kids the fire engine."

"What?" Bridget sat there with her mouth open in shock. "You never mentioned him before."

"I'm sorry I never told you earlier. I thought I wouldn't see him again."

Bridget smiled then said, "That's all right, I suppose I would have been the same. So what are you going to do?" Bridget asked, now eager to know every detail of her friend's new admirer.

"I'm not sure… will you come up with me?"

"Yes, I will! What you going to say to him?"

"Not sure let's go now before Johnny comes back."

Sylvia thought she had nothing to lose. As they were walking closer to the fire engine, Sylvia's tummy was doing somersaults. When they got there, Gregg made a bees line towards Sylvia; it seemed she'd had nothing to worry about.

"Hi, how you been? Haven't seen you out for a while," Gregg said while glancing at Sylvia.

"Well, I've been about."

"We must have been two ships in the night." Sylvia just laughed.

Then Gregg asked if she would be out tonight. Trying not to be too eager she said, "I think we are out, aren't we Bridget?" Bridget was just looking like she was watching a film at The Majestic.

Sylvia nudged her.

"Oh! Yes, we will."

"That's all right then. Got a mate to keep you company," Gregg laughed. Bridget wasn't sure if he was joking or serious. She just laughed nervously. "See you in The Old Slipper around 8 o'clock then?"

"See you tonight," Sylvia said as she and Bridget turned around and went back down by the oak tree. Sylvia was feeling like she was on cloud nine.

"I can't believe what just happened, you got a date! Good looking as well."

Bridget was pleased for Sylvia.

"Don't forget you've got a date as well!" Sylvia reminded Bridget.

"Are you sure he meant he was bringing someone? I don't want to be standing around like a gooseberry all night." Bridget started to have doubts.

"No, you won't feel like that, I'm pretty sure he is bringing someone," Sylvia said, trying to make Bridget feel better. "Let's just enjoy ourselves tonight and not worry about anything." Sylvia couldn't wait to meet Gregg later.

CHAPTER TWENTY

When Annie, Wilma, Mable and their families went back with their food they, sat where they had been before.

Not long after, Frank, Gilbert and Henry went over to where Annie was sitting with the others. "We are off to The Running Hare with Sid and Johnny," Frank said while glancing at Annie.

"I don't know why you're telling us; we're not your keepers!"

"You can do what you like, Pet." Annie gave a faint smile.

"Well, we'll see you girls later then." Frank said as they walked away.

"Well, I say, did you see that look?" Wilma said as she ate her sandwich.

"See what look?"

"That look from Frank. He couldn't keep his eyes off you?" Wilma was all excited. By now Annie realised what Wilma was talking about.

Mable then said, "I saw the look too. He definitely likes you, Annie."

As Annie was excited about Frank, everyone forgot for a moment that their Mums were sat listening to everything. Suddenly, Annie's mum said, "We all think so too." Annie, Wilma and Mable just looked at each other, then laughed with their mums.

Soon after, the talks turned to the murder of Brian Dent and if the police had any leads "I think the police haven't got a clue to who killed him," Annie was the first to speak. "It could be anyone from the factory, as nearly everyone despised him he was a piece of shit!"

"Annie mind your language!" Annie's mum said in a firm voice.

"Sorry Mum, but he was."

"I dare say he was, but you don't speak ill of the dead." Annie's Mum spoke in a firm voice, "Can we get back to Frank, please?" she said, realising her daughter was trying to change the subject.

"Yes, Annie we know Frank likes you," Mable says to Annie.

"The killer could be here at the picnic, eating our food. How sick is that?" Wilma feeling slightly nervy as she ate her last sandwich couldn't let the topic drop.

"I think it isn't worth being scared all the time, else we wouldn't want to go to the factory at all." Annie was trying to be realistic, "All I'm saying is, Brian was killed because he was a horrible person, the chances one of us will is low."

"Annie don't be a wishful thinker," Mable reminded her.

CHAPTER TWENTY-ONE

As it was a Saturday and Manchester United was playing Liverpool at home, The Running Hare was packed for the 3 o'clock kick off. The radio was on in the corner so everyone in the pub could listen to the score.

Johnny had just got the first-round in. Everyone was in good spirits as they listened to the match. With it being so busy Johnny, Sid, Henry, Frank and Gilbert had to stand. "At least standing at the bar, makes it easier to get the drinks in," Johnny said.

It wasn't long until the murder came up in conversation. Frank was the first to ask the others if they had any idea who might have killed Brian Sid just stared at the others then went on to say, "It could have been anyone in the factory. I bet the police will be back on Monday."

"The times they have questioned us, seems like the police haven't a clue who it is," Johnny said whilst taking a sip of his beer.

As the first goal came in for Manchester United, there was a massive cheer. 1-0 to Manchester after half an hour of play. As the cheering fans calmed down a man called Jim West walked into the pub - Vera Jones' brother-in-law. He was standing at the back, when there was loud cheer: United had just scored again.

After the second goal, Jim saw a gap at the back and started to squeeze his way through the supporters. After he managed to order his drink, he scanned the room to see what was going on. To his surprise he thought he saw someone he knew. He looked back again and couldn't believe his eyes. He started to go white and sweaty as if he'd seen a ghost! Then as quick as the wind, he was gone from the pub before he had chance to finish his pint.

Johnny went to stand by Sid, "When do you think we could sell some more parts?" Johnny pushed Sid for an answer again.

Not long after, Sid pulled Johnny to one side and quietly told him, "Look, I may be able to get the parts. I just remembered the police are gone by lunch time. But it will be the last, then I'm done for good. How many can you take?"

Johnny looked puzzled. "How come you changed your mind?"

"It's because I have got quite a few out the back of the factory to get rid of. Then that's it." Johnny nodded. By half time the score was 3-0 to Manchester United and everyone in the pub was cheering them on.

CHAPTER TWENTY-TWO

While Sylvia and Bridget were listening to the music on the radio. Vera from the office came along. "How are you doing? Having a good time? I wanted to introduce my sister, Jane. She has come up from London with her husband. They are staying at my place, for the weekend."

"That's nice to have your sister, I mean, Jane staying with you," Sylvia chirped as she tried to make conversation. Vera was the sort of person that liked to know your business but would not tell you about herself.

"I didn't know you had a sister, Vera?" Bridget said, trying to make a point.

"Oh yes dear, didn't I mention it at work?"

"No, I don't think you did," Bridget replied.

"I think it is nice for our company to organise these days out, do you think so girls?" Sylvia and Bridget just nodded and smiled. "I think we will make a move now and go home, it has been a tiring day," Vera said as she and her sister walked on.

After they left Bridget moaned, "I should have known the men would have snuck off to the pub."

"What do you expect when United are playing at home?" Sylvia was not surprised at all. "We won't see them again today. At least it has been a lovely day."

"I guess we should help clear the food away?" Bridget suggested. Sylvia, feeling tired, eventually got up to help the other women.

"What ever shall we do with all this food that is left?" Bridget was surprised there was so much food left over.

"I think it be best we share it all out amongst ourselves," Suzi said, while trying to keep her kids in check.

"It's all right for the men, they're in the pub," Annie agreed as she started sharing the sandwiches and sausage rolls out to everyone. By the time they had cleared away the food most of the folk had left the park.

Sylvia and Bridget were glad they were heading home, they were both tired after a fun day. "By the time we get home we will have to get ready to go out again," Sylvia moaned to Bridget.

"I wonder who he brings with him, I hope I like him or it will be a shit night for me!" Bridget was feeling anxious about going. "Perhaps I'm feeling tired after the long day."

Sylvia was now worried in case Bridget didn't like her blind date and would decide not to come. "Don't worry about me. At least you got your date and I suppose it was nice of Gregg to think of me." Bridget said, knowing it was an important night for Sylvia.

"Let's hope the union doesn't organise another

picnic so soon next time. I am beat." Bridget sighed as she leaned her head on Sylvia's shoulder.

"We should feel better after we take a bath and get changed," Sylvia said, trying to be optimistic.

"I feel sorry for Suzi. I hear she is always left to look after the kids on her own. I want a man that is there for me, not in the pub all the time."

"I feel the same, Bridget, I think a marriage works both ways." When their bus reached their stop, they both made their way home.

CHAPTER TWENTY-THREE

As soon as Sylvia got home, she went straight up to her bedroom to lie on her bed. As she was wore out from her day at the picnic. Not long after Sylvia's mum shouted from the top of the stairs. "I take it you and Bridget had a good time at the picnic?"

Sylvia thought it would be better to go downstairs, rather than shout from her bedroom. Once she made her way to the kitchen. Where her mum was making tea. Sylvia told her mum all about what happened at the picnic. Even her date with Greig.

After filling in her mum about her day. Sylvia had her tea with her mum and dad before getting ready for her date. After Sylvia had her bath, she started to feel nervous in meeting Greig. Trying not to think too much on it she finished getting dressed, then she made her way downstairs, as she arranged to meet Bridget at the bus stop for 7 o'clock.

"I'm leaving now mum; I won't be too late home" Sylvia shouted as she left the house. As she walked to the bus stop, she could see Bridget waiting. "I should have known you be here first" Sylvia said while lighting a cigarette. "I just thought we better be on time, being a first date and all." Sylvia just looked at Bridget and laughed. "Trust you to say that." Sylvia then shook her head.

After they had been waiting a few minutes, the bus came. Once on the bus Sylvia admitted to Bridget that she was nervous in meeting Greig. "I could do with a few Gin and Tonics right now" Bridget laughed then said. "To be honest I'm feeling a bit nervous myself and I don't even know who I am meeting" both girls started to laugh. "You always say the right thing" Sylvia put her head on Bridget's shoulder then said. "I think we will be alright when we get into the pub and have a few drinks." "Yes, we will" Bridget replied.

Once Sylvia and Bridget got off the bus, they made their way to The Running Hare. By now the clock struck 7.30pm. When in the pub, Sylvia looked round to see if Greig was in there, but there was no sign he was there yet. The pub was still busy after the football match that afternoon. "Let's get some drinks in us before they turn up," Bridget told Sylvia.

Then just as Sylvia and Bridget was getting a second round in Greig and Ben walked into the pub. Soon as Greig saw Sylvia and Bridget he went straight over to talk to them. "Hi, you two been here long?" Greig asked Sylvia. "No, we haven't been here long" Sylvia replied. "Let me introduce Ben, Ben this is Bridget" "Nice to meet you Ben" Bridget could feel herself go red in the face, so she looked away.

Once all four got their drinks Sylvia suggested to sit at a table by the window.

"So where would you ladies like to go after here?" Greig said, trying to make conversation.

"I know, shall we go round the fair its only here for tonight," Bridget asked everyone.

"Yes, that's a good idea maybe we could go to another pub first, if that's alright?" Sylvia waited for an answer.

"Well, that settles it, the fair it is," Greig said as he glanced at Sylvia.

After having a few more drinks Greig, Ben, Bridget and Sylvia started to get to know each other. With a few more drinks all four were more relaxed. By now The Running Hare was getting packed, so Greig suggested, "It may be a good idea we go now to The Old Hag with it getting so crowded in here" Sylvia and Bridget agreed with Greig.

Just as Greig, Sylvia, Bridget and Ben were leaving Johnny and Henry walked in The Running Hare. "Hey there, how's my favourite girls doing?" Johnny asked. It was obvious that Johnny had had a few too many drinks.

"We are fine Johnny, we may see you later, are you going to the fair?" Sylvia asked.

"We may do, see how we get on," Johnny replied.

"I think Johnny has had a few too many. That is our friend Johnny, he works with us at All Parts," Bridget told Greig and Ben.

When Sylvia, Ben, Bridget and Sylvia reached the Old Hag it was starting to get dark. With the fair in town it meant there was a lot of folk about.

When Greig got the next round of drinks in, all four went to sit at a table near the door. By now everyone was getting on really well, especially Sylvia and Greig.

"Shall we go to the fair now?" Sylvia suggested.

Sylvia, Greig, Bridget and Ben walked towards the fair. It was a sight to see, with all the lights flashing and young folk screaming on the rides. With the music playing made it feel even more exciting. The first stop was the coconut stand; Greig and Ben both won teddies for the girls.

Next was the slide with Sylvia on Greig's lap and Bridget on Ben's. They were really having fun. But in the dark, there was someone watching from a distance. People walking by minding their own business to what this person was thinking and doing. Watching every move Sylvia and Bridget was making. Is anyone safe from the office or is it just a waiting game till the killer strikes again.

CHAPTER TWENTY-FOUR

By Monday morning Sylvia was up earlier than usual. Meeting Gregg on the Saturday night had gone really well - even Gregg's friend Ben got on with Bridget. They got on so well they are both meeting them the next Saturday night.

Sylvia was so happy that she didn't care it was Monday.

As Sylvia went down the stairs, she could hear her mum in the kitchen and when she opened the kitchen door, her mum asked if she wanted a cooked breakfast.

"Oh, and a cuppa, that would be great, Mum."

After Sylvia had eaten her breakfast she made her way to the bus stop. Up ahead she could see Bridget waiting.

A few minutes after, the bus came. Sylvia and Bridget found a seat and sat down. They both lit a cigarette. As usual the bus was packed, they were lucky to find somewhere to sit.

Not long after Sylvia and Bridget got on the bus, a

work colleague, Bob, said, "Have you two heard the local news this morning?"

"No, I haven't. Why?" Sylvia wondered what the old chap was on about.

"Well, there's been another murder, this time the news says it was brutal. It happened late last night in a park." Sylvia and Bridget were shocked when the old chap said a park. Sylvia tried to get more out of Bob, but he didn't know anything else.

As soon as the bus stopped outside the factory Sylvia and Bridget made their way to the office. There, a few of the workers were standing drinking their tea. Sylvia asked Ken, "What has happened?"

"Vera was found murdered in Heaton Park late last night." Sylvia's face dropped. She could not believe what she'd just heard. Bridget just stood there in shock. Sylvia pushed Ken for more. " Apparently she was walking back home from bingo, she always took a short cut through Heaton Park. It was brutal, a number of blows to the head, that is all I know."

"Two murders in two weeks, who will be next?" Bridget mumbled whilst pouring another cup of tea for Sylvia and herself. A few minutes later Johnny came through the door.

"I just heard off Mr. Mortimer. I can't believe it! Poor Vera, she never deserved that."

Then Sylvia remembered that Vera had her sister and brother-in-law up for the weekend. "I hope they are alright." Everyone in the office was in shock.

Then Mr Mortimer came in the office. "I know it has been a shock hearing this terrible news about Miss

Jones. So, I want everyone in this office to go home for today. With pay of course. It is only right to do so."

When Mr. Mortimer left, everyone in the office was surprised they had been given the day off. A short time after, they all started to leave the office.

"Me and Sylvia are going to the café, are you coming?"

"Yeah, I will join you in a minute, just need to see someone," Johnny shouted over to Bridget.

After leaving Johnny, Sylvia and Bridget made their way to the café. Bridget went to order two coffees and two rounds of toast. Sandra, the waitress could not stop going on about the murder, asking all sorts of questions. Bridget wasn't listening all that much to what Sandra was going on about. As soon as Bridget got her order she went to sit next to Sylvia. "Did you hear that nosy Sandra going on? She does my head in," Bridget moaned to Sylvia. "So where did Vera live?" Bridget asked Sylvia.

"I think she lived up by the church, Oak View I think."

"Why Vera? She was harmless, always kept to herself." Sipping her coffee, Bridget gave Sylvia a strange look.

"Why ever you looking at me strange for?"

"I was wondering who will be next? Two been murdered now from the office," Bridget was starting to get scared.

Just then Johnny burst through the door. "I'll get my own, shall I?" Johnny smiled then winked at Sylvia and Bridget.

"We would have got yours, but we didn't know how long you were going to be!" Sylvia shouted over to Johnny. When Johnny joined Sylvia and Bridget, he told them it was only the office staff who had the day off.

While putting money in the jukebox Bridget shouted over to Sylvia and Johnny. "We only just saw Vera at the picnic on Saturday, she was with her sister."

"I didn't even know she had a sister!" Johnny seemed surprised.

"Her name is Jane from London. She came up with her husband for the weekend."

After Bridget picked which songs, she wanted on the jukebox she went to sit down by Sylvia. Johnny quietly said, "Don't worry ladies, you got me to protect you both."

"Well, that is always good to know. Now, you can start by buying us two ladies another coffee!" Sylvia laughed whilst handing the two cups to Johnny.

"Right, two coffees coming up." Sylvia and Bridget always felt safe when they were with Johnny.

While he was getting the drinks in, Sandra was asking him all kinds of questions about the murder of Vera Jones. "How would I know how and where Vera was murdered? Have some respect!" Johnny was starting to lose his temper with Sandra, she never shut up. She was the sort who wanted to know everything but never told you anything about herself.

When Johnny paid for the coffees, he made his way back to his seat. "That woman makes me mad asking all these questions about the murder. She is so nosy."

"Take no notice of her, she needs putting down a

peg or two," Sylvia said giving Sandra an evil stare. Not letting Sandra spoil things, the three carried on drinking their coffees and listening to the music on the jukebox.

"In a way the café is much better when it isn't busy," Sylvia pointed out to Johnny and Bridget.

"When I came in, two police cars turned up," Johnny informed Sylvia and Bridget.

"I hope the police don't come to my house" Bridget worried as she ate her toast. "Why kill Vera she wouldn't hurt a fly? It doesn't make sense!"

CHAPTER TWENTY-FIVE

While the Inspector was asleep in his bed the phone rang, it was 4.30am as he glanced at the clock. He had a strange feeling even before he answered the phone. Rightly so, there had been another murder. After taking notes the Inspector got dressed, trying not to wake his wife.

PC Lamb told the Inspector he would meet him at the scene of the murder Heaton Park. When the Inspector arrived PC Lamb and PC Spencer were at the scene. Lamb updated the Inspector who the deceased was and that she lived not far from here at 10 Oak View Crescent.

PC Lamb pointed out who Miss Vera Jones was. As the Inspector looked, he couldn't believe she worked at All Parts the same as Brian Dent; it had to be connected. "Apparently Miss Jones was on her way home from bingo. She usually takes a short cut through the park to her house, which isn't too far from here, Gov."

The Inspector knelt to take a closer look at the

body. "The Doctor says Miss Jones was hit three times on the back of the head. Maybe with a bat of some sort, she would have died instantly. With how much blood there is and with the force of the blows. A dog walker found her early this morning. The Doctor thinks she'd probably been dragged behind these bushes. The walker only found her because he chucked a ball for the dog to fetch. Then the dog just barked 'til the man came to see what the dog was barking at."

Inspector then asked PC Lamb, "Was there any evidence near the body?"

PC Lamb replied. "Yes, there was Gov, a cinema ticket with blood on, and a cigarette butt. We bagged them up."

"Did the cinema ticket have a time and a date? Oh, and at which cinema was it?"

PC Lamb told the Inspector, "The cinema ticket had a date which was the 8th of April, and it was for the Majestic. There was no weapon near the body. Two PCs have also searched the grounds with no luck."

Inspector Wright thought for a moment "Why would someone murder her? Did she see someone the night Mr Dent was killed?"

"Whoever it was they meant to kill her, how hard they hit her. Not just once but three times. With all the blood the killer must have had a rage on them."

"Who was her next of kin?"

"I believe she had a sister who lives in London, and I believe she lived alone Gov"

"The Doctor says they are ready to take the body to

the mortuary now, there will be a post-mortem later today." PC Spencer told the Inspector.

Inspector Wright then reminded PC Spencer to let the Police in London know of the murder of Vera Jones, so they can inform her sister being murdered.

When the Inspector and PC Lamb arrived at Vera's house, there was a small crowd forming outside. "Could you please go home? There is nothing you can do here."

After PC Lamb cleared the people away, the Inspector got a key that had been found in Vera's handbag out to open the front door. As Miss Vera Jones, lived alone and her next of kin her sister lived in London, the Inspector knew the house would be empty. First the Inspector went into the living room, everything seemed to be in place. It was the same in all the other rooms as well. There were a few letters on the kitchen table, looked like bills mostly. After having a look round Vera's home, the Inspector decided to go back to the factory. He thought he would question the manager and the office staff Vera worked with.

When the Inspector and PC Lamb arrived at the factory, he was told the office staff Vera worked with were given the day of. An inconvenience, but he could understand why they must have all been very shaken. He took the opportunity to once again question the manager instead.

"On Friday last, how did Miss Jones seem to you?"

The manager thought for a moment then replied, "Miss Jones seemed like her usual self. I know she was looking forward to going to the works picnic because she told me the last time, I saw her. We have the first picnic in April, then we have another in May. Then every month until autumn, depending on the weather forecast. If it is raining on the day of the picnic, it gets cancelled 'til the following month."

"Do you go on the picnic Mr Mortimer?"

"Sometimes I do go with my wife, but we never this time. I still can't believe two people from the same office have been murdered. That is why I gave the office staff the day off, it was only right."

"I will come back tomorrow and question them. Oh, lastly Mr Mortimer where were you from 10pm yesterday evening?"

"Well, I was at home with my wife, all evening"

"Thank you for that Mr Mortimer, we will be in touch" The Inspector and PC Lamb then decided to head back to the station.

CHAPTER TWENTY-SIX

By the next morning, the Inspector was more than ready to go back to the factory and question the office workers. He knew he would catch a break sooner or later. He just had to be patient. All the clues were there in front of him. He just needed to put them together. As soon as the Inspector finished his breakfast, he was ready to go back to the factory.

A few minutes later, PC Lamb was waiting outside his front door in the car for the Inspector. When they arrived at the factory, it was 8.30am. "All the workers should be here by now," the Inspector thought out loud as he checked his watch. Not wasting another minute, they went straight to the office where everyone was working and called the first person in for questioning.

First the Inspector decided to question Mr Ken Rollings who sorts out all the shipping. When PC Lamb brought in Mr Rollings, the Inspector asked him to take a seat. "Yesterday Miss Vera Jones was found dead in Heaton Park. We believe she was murdered between

10.30pm to 11.30pm after she'd left the bingo hall. Miss Jones then took a short cut through Heaton Park to her home. We know she was alive just after 10 o'clock. That was the last time anyone saw her at the bingo hall that night. When was the last time you saw or spoke to Miss Jones?" The Inspector waited for an answer.

"Well, it must have been at the picnic Saturday just gone. It was busy as the weather was good for this time of year. Me and my wife, Jenny, was sat on the grass with Vera and her sister Jane I think her name was. most of the day they stayed with me and my wife. Vera's sister had come up to visit with her husband from London. They had come up for the weekend."

"Before you go Mr Rollings, where were you from 10pm last evening?"

"I was at home all evening with my wife".

"I think that will be all for now, Mr Rollings." PC Lamb then led Mr. Rollings out of the office.—Miss Bridget Molt was in next.

The Inspector asked Miss Molt to take a seat. "Could you tell me when the last time you saw or spoke to Miss Jones?"

"I believe the last time myself and Sylvia saw and spoke to Miss Jones, was at the picnic. She seemed happy as her sister was staying with her for the weekend."

"What time would that have been, Miss Molt?"

"It must have been around 5.15pm. Everyone was starting to go home. Me and Sylvia stayed to help clear everything away and sort all the food that was left over."

"I think that will be all for now Miss Molt."

As before PC Lamb brought in Miss Sylvia Weston. "Please take a seat Miss Weston, in your own time could you tell me, when was the last time you saw or spoke to Miss Jones?"

Sylvia thought for a moment then said, "It was at the picnic Vera was with her sister who was staying with her husband for the weekend. She seemed happy."

"Miss Molt did say that you were with her when you both spoke to Miss Jones." Sylvia confirmed this then asked the Inspector if he had any leads on the case? The Inspector replied, "No not at this time. Last question, Miss Weston. Do you know of anyone who would have harmed Miss Jones?"

Sylvia was trying to make sense of the question put to her. She then said "No, no one. Miss Jones was a lovely lady. She would go out of her way to help you."

"Well, I think that will be all for now, Miss Weston."

After Sylvia left the office, PC Lamb brought Mr Johnny Hill in next. Johnny was the last one in the office to be questioned. "Please take a seat, Mr Hill. Could you tell me when the last time you saw or spoke to Miss Jones?"

After lighting a cigarette Johnny thought, then said. "It must have been on Friday, when Miss Jones wanted to ask me about some paperwork."

"Could you tell me in more detail, Mr Hill?"

"Well, it was about an order Vera thought she had ordered two instead of one. She wanted me to check the invoices to see if there was a double order of the same thing. But when I checked there was just one order. That was the last I saw of Miss Jones."

"I think that will be all for now, Mr Hill."

Just after Johnny left the office, a phone call came in for the Inspector from the Chief of Police.–The post-mortem had been done. Also, there was evidence that came back from the lab. There was a blood stain which was B positive on the cinema ticket. Miss Jones' blood type was A positive. Lastly Miss Jones' sister and brother-in-law had arrived from London. They would be staying at Miss Jones' house. "I will give you more details when you return to the station."

The trouble was that the Inspector would have to prove the cinema ticket was dropped by the killer. The Inspector needed to get firm evidence if he wanted to catch the killer. He knew that it wouldn't be enough to hold someone. Did Miss Jones cut the killer in some way?

After the Inspector had finished his questioning, he was still no wiser as to who killed Mr Dent and Miss Jones. He and PC Lamb headed back to the station to question Miss Jones' sister and brother-in-law. That was the next step, but where would the Inspector go from there?

CHAPTER TWENTY-SEVEN

Just as Annie packed her last box, the bell went for home time. Wilma and Mable were ready to clock out - they were just waiting for Annie to finish her last box. When Annie finished, she, Wilma and Mable went to clock out for the day. "Before we go home, let's go for a coffee?" Annie suggested.

As soon as they were ready Annie, Wilma and Mable went to the café to unwind. It was not long until the café was filling up with the factory workers.

Sid was on the vender machine opposite the jukebox where he'd just won the jackpot. "Don't put any more money in now you have won, else it will take it all back again!" Annie shouted over to Sid. After Sid finished on the vender machine, he came over to talk to Annie.

"Were you interviewed by the police today?"

"No, just the office workers were interviewed today. Even if I were, I couldn't really tell them much. I didn't see Vera at the picnic last Saturday - I think she was with her sister. Did they interview you, Sid?"

"No, they never asked me to be questioned."

"Same here, I only saw Vera at a distance as I went with the other lads to The Running Hare to hear the football match on the radio. Can't wait to go and watch Manchester United play against Arsenal on the 26th of April, it should be a good match."

"What was the score last Saturday then? While you lads were in the pubs leaving us girls on our own," Annie teased trying to wind Sid up.

4 - 0 to United. It would have been a good match to watch but can't afford to watch them all. Well, I better be off else my tea will be in the dog!" Sid said with a wink and left the café.

Just as Annie got some more drinks, Frank and Gilbert came in. She hurried back to her seat and trying desperately not to make it obvious, but she did go red when she saw Frank come in the café.

"Annie, you have gone bright red!" Wilma teased as she drank her coffee.

"Don't make things worse! Yes, I have gone red. I always do when I see Frank. What's wrong with me!"

"There's nothing wrong with you, you just fancy him," Mable said supportively.

"I'm going to put some more songs on the jukebox." Just as "My foolish heart" Billy Eckstine came on. Annie started to sing to it while she chose some more songs. Suddenly someone came up behind her, to her surprise it was Frank. Annie turned round quickly; as she picked another song, she thought at least he couldn't see her go red.

"Hope you're picking some good songs."

Annie blushed then spoke. "Well, you will know in a minute, won't you?"

When Annie turned round, Frank was smiling. "Well, I just wanted to ask you if you would like to come out this Saturday? To the Crystal Rooms?" Annie could feel herself go red, so she turned away hoping he never noticed. She was so surprised - she'd never seen that coming at all.

"Yes, I will go out with you on Saturday. Where and what time did you have in mind?"

"I was thinking 7.30pm outside the Majestic. Will that be all right with you?"

"Yes, I will be there for 7.30pm Saturday."

Annie was still in a daze; she could not believe Frank had asked her out. She had almost given up hope. "Will Wilma and Mable be going to the Crystal Rooms?" Frank asked.

"I think they will be going."

"It's just that Gilbert likes Wilma, and my cousin Bobby is sweet on Mable."

"Oh my, that's a lot to take in, but I do believe it can work." Annie's mind was racing with all that information, but that it was sweet of Frank to think of Wilma and Mable. So, they would not be left out. Most men wouldn't have cared.

"So, I will see you Saturday then?"

"Yes, looking forward to it."

As soon as Frank and Gilbert had left the café, Annie rushed back to her seat to tell Wilma and Mable what Frank had said. They were speechless! They both thought Annie was having them on at first.

"You do like Gilbert don't you Wilma?"

"Yes, I do but, I didn't say anything because I never thought he liked me."

"Never mind that, he will see you up at the Crystal Rooms. I think he was too shy to ask you out in person." Annie then noticed Mable was very quiet. "What's wrong?"

"I think I know Franks cousin; his name is Bobby Billings?"

"Yes, that's right, he ain't half bad, so do you like him?" Annie asked hoping, she does.

"Do you need to ask? Yes, I do like him! You sure Frank said that? You're not having me on?"

"No, I'm not having you on, you know I wouldn't do that to you. You're a beautiful woman, why shouldn't he like you?" Annie and the girls were in good spirits singing along to the songs. All this time, Frank really did like Annie.

CHAPTER TWENTY-EIGHT

When the Inspector returned to the police station, the Chief asked him to go to his office.

"This time the killer was more brutal, she was stabbed once in the back of the neck. It may have been the same knife that the killer used on Mr Dent. There were three blows to her head consisting to an over kill. By the look of the injuries, the weapon could have been something like a cricket bat. We need to catch this killer, before they kill again!"

Listening to the Chief, the Inspector knew he had to think like the killer to catch him - or her. So, before the Inspector went home for the night, he decided to go over the interview notes. There must have been something the Inspector wasn't seeing.

After many hours going through the notes on both murders, the Inspector called it a night and went home. All the way home the Inspector had a feeling he was overlooking something. Something that would break the case!

The next morning the Inspector was up early. He wanted to question Miss Jones' sister and brother-in-law. As usual PC Lamb was waiting outside for him. When the Inspector was ready, they went straight over to Miss Jones' house where her sister and brother-in-law were staying.

When PC Lamb knocked on the door, Jim answered then showed PC Lamb and the Inspector into the living room.

"Please take a seat." Jim asked the Inspector and PC Lamb, "Have you caught the killer?" Mr West was eager to know.

"Not at this time. Before I ask you anything, I just would like to say how sorry we are for your loss. We will do everything we can to catch, whoever killed your sister-in-law"

"We understand, Mr West you identified Miss Jones this morning?"

"Yes, I did," Mr West replied.

The Inspector asked Mr West if it was possible to speak with is wife.

Jim West then told the Inspector, "My wife is up stairs in her room, and she was to upset to speak to anyone at the moment"

"I understand Mr West. I'm hoping you can answer some questions for me."

"I just want to ask on Saturday April 12th when your sister in law went to the picnic, how was your sister in law?"

"Well Vera was in a good mood, with it being a lovely sunny day for the time of year. I believe she sat with a co-worker and his wife. I think his name was Ken."

The Inspector then asked, "When was the last time you saw and spoke to your sister-in-law"

"That was Sunday afternoon, we left around 3 o'clock when we headed back to London. I believe she was going to bingo that evening."

"Thank you for that information, we will keep you posted with any new developments"

From there, the Inspector and PC Lamb went straight to the factory to question the office workers to find out who was in contact with Vera Jones. As the second murder was connected with Brian's murder, and being from the same office, the Inspector knew he needed to solve this case very soon, before there was another murder. He also knew to put more pressure on the workers of All Parts as one of them had to know something.

In the same office as before, the Inspector asked PC Lamb to bring in the first worker, which was Miss Bridget Molt.

When Miss Molt entered the office, the Inspector asked her to take a seat. As she sat, Inspector Wright sat opposite gazing pointedly, trying to make Miss Molt feel uncomfortable.

"I am here today to ask everyone who worked with Miss Jones and Mr Dent further questions. Were you aware that Miss Jones went to bingo on a Sunday night?"

Miss Molt thought for a moment then said, "Yes, I am aware Miss Jones goes... went to bingo. I often saw her there when I went with my Mum. But I never went this Sunday as I was to knackered after the weekend. Else I would have seen her there."

"Do you know anyone else that goes to the bingo?"

"Well Sylvia goes with her mum most weeks; I think Johnny goes sometimes. I also have seen Sid with his wife and some of the packers go also."

"Just one last question, where were you this last Sunday from 10pm?"

"Oh, I was at home in my room reading"

"Thank you I think that will be all for now, Miss Molt."

The Inspector was intrigued as there were quite a few workers who went to bingo when Miss Jones did.

So, when the next person entered his small office, the Inspector asked Miss Sylvia Weston to take a seat. "Were you at bingo on Sunday evening?" The Inspector asked.

"Yes, I did go to bingo with my mum. We weren't going to go but we changed our minds."

"Oh, I see Did you see Miss Jones there?"

Sylvia went quiet, she realised the other day she told the Inspector that the last time she saw Vera was on Saturday at the picnic. Putting her hand to her mouth, she then told the Inspector. "I am sorry, I forgot we went to bingo."

"Let us not get into that now, did you see Miss Jones at the bingo hall on Sunday evening?"

"Yes. Only when we arrived at the bingo hall, I never saw her again."

"Did you notice if Miss Jones was on her own or

with someone else?" The Inspector by now was starting to lose his patience.

"I think she was on her own, she usually was."

"So, what time did you leave the bingo hall?"

"It was just after 10pm. I know because I remember glancing at my watch"

"That has been very helpful, Miss Weston. I think that will do for now."

The Inspector called for Mr Holmes next. When Sid walked in, he was asked to take a seat opposite the Inspector. "Mr Holmes were you at bingo last Sunday evening?"

Sid thought for a moment. "Yes, I did go to the bingo with the Missus."

"Right, I see Mr. Holmes. So did you see or speak with Miss Jones while you were at the bingo?"

"No, I didn't speak to her, but - now you mention it - I did see her there"

"Mr Holmes was she on her own?"

"Yes, I think she was on her own"

"Last question, what time was it when you saw Miss Jones?"

"It was after bingo when we were all leaving, so that was after 10 o'clock. Also, we saw Johnny - I mean Mr Hill - he was in front of us when we were leaving."

"Thank you, Mr Holmes. I think that will be all for now".

The last one on the list was Mr Johnny Hill. When PC Lamb brought him in, the Inspector said, "Just a few questions Mr Hill. Did you go to bingo on Sunday last?"

Lighting a cigarette, Johnny said, "Yes, I did go to

bingo on Sunday, but I didn't play. I just went for a few pints before going to the local pubs. The bingo hall opens an hour before the pubs do. I do play bingo sometimes, mostly if I go with Sylvia and Bridget."

"Did you see Miss Jones at the bingo hall?"

"No. Like I said, I was only there a short while. Anyhow the bingo hadn't even started when I was there." The Inspector paused for a moment then asked. "It may be a strange question, Mr. Hill, but did you go to the cinema last Sunday?"

Johnny stared at the Inspector then said, "Yes, I did go to the cinema last Sunday" Johnny was surprised the Inspector asked that question.

"Finally, Mr Hill, where did you go after you were at the bingo hall?"

"Oh, I went to have a few pints in The Running Hare, 'till about 10.30pm. Then I walked home."

"Did anyone you know see you in The Running Hare?"

"No, I don't think so. It was packed in there, but I don't remember seeing anyone I know."

"I think that will be all for now, Mr Hill."

When the Inspector had finished questioning the workers, he and PC Lamb headed back to the police station. Out of nowhere the Inspector had an idea: the torch that was left by the side of Mr Dent's body had been checked for prints, but the batteries inside may have fingerprints on them.

Wasting no time, the Inspector rang through to the evidence room to get the batteries checked for fingerprints. Even though there may be none, the

Inspector knew it is worth a shot. He may get lucky. For now, the murderer has been careful not to be found, but maybe they hadn't thought of everything. The Inspector also knew it had to be someone from the factory that was being blackmailed by Mr Dent who killed him, but what about Vera Jones? She was a different story. Most people seemed to like her, so why was she murdered? Did she find out something that cost her her life?

On 4th April Mr Brian Dent was found dead in the manager's office by the caretaker Bill Mills. Mr Dent was found face down, with a single stab wound to the heart. Left by his body, a rubber glove and a torch. There was no knife left at the scene and could have - most probably - been the same knife to stab Miss Jones in the neck before she was beaten. The other weapon may have been a cricket bat used on Miss Jones but was not at the scene either.

From Mr Dent's post-mortem, it showed he was murdered in the early hours of the morning. Which left a two-hour doorway around 3am.

While the Inspector was looking through the case notes he got thinking about the other case he'd worked in London. There was something making the Inspector think the two cases were familiar, but why?

Not long after, the Inspector called for PC Lamb to arrange to speak with Miss Jones' sister and brother in-law again.

When the Inspector and PC Lamb arrived at Miss Jones' house, they knocked on the front door. After a few moments, the door opened. It was Mr West. "Have you any news, Inspector?"

"Not at this moment, Mr West. May we come in?" The Inspector and PC Lamb made their way into the living room where Mrs West was sitting in a chair.

"Please take a seat, would you both like a cup of tea?"

"No thank you Mrs West." The Inspector went on to say, "I am here to ask you a few questions about another matter." Mr. and Mrs. West wondered what the question would be about. "Do you know anyone who came from London to Manchester in these last few years? I know it is a strange question, but I assure you it is important you answer honestly."

Mr West went quiet then gave his wife a strange look. Then Mr. West, said," No, not who I can think of. What has this got to do with Vera's murder?"

Mrs West also seemed somewhat confused by the question. "So, you think a Londoner may have killed Vera?"

"We are not sure at this point, Mrs West, just clearing up loose ends." The Inspector did not want to say too much in case he was wrong. "I think that will be all for now Mr and Mrs West. Thank you for your time." Inspector Wright and PC Lamb said they will show themselves out. "But, if you do think of something, please let me know."

CHAPTER TWENTY-NINE

At the factory Annie, Wilma and Mable were in good spirits as it was Friday. They were all excited about going to the Crystal Rooms on the Saturday night.

Annie still could not believe she was going on a date with Frank. She had liked him since she started working at All Parts over two years ago. Annie almost had given up hope that Frank would ever ask her out on a date.

"Will you be going out tonight Annie?" Wilma asked while boxing the parts.

"I thought we could wait to go out on Saturday, but if you two want to go out that's fine with me. Also, I've got a few chores to do tonight."

"No, you're right, let's wait 'till tomorrow to go out. Is that alright with you Mable?"

"Yes, that be fine by me. Anyhow my mum wanted me to watch my kid sister and brother so she can go to bingo tonight."

"What about you Wilma, are you going anywhere tonight?"

"I may go to bingo with my mum. See how I feel after tea."

"We can make up for it by having a good time tomorrow night," Annie smiled.

Glancing at the clock, the three of them only had an hour left before the bell went for home time. "At least we have the weekend off." Annie felt beat after reaching her target for the day. "After we clock out, shall we go to the café? Put some songs on the jukebox and that can be our low-key Friday night." Wilma and Mable agreed with Annie.

In the café Annie went up to the counter, to put an order in. "I will have three coffees and two rounds of toast for three, please."

"Any more news on the murders Annie?" Sandra asked while getting Annie's orders ready.

"No more news, only the office has been interviewed twice now, the police must think it is one of them."

"I feel sorry for you lot, being in the middle of it all." Sandra said, while giving Annie her order on a tray.

As soon as Annie got to where Wilma and Mable were sitting, it was not long until the conversation started back on their dates for the following evening.

"Do you two fancy going clothes shopping tomorrow?" Wilma asked.

Annie and Mable thought for a moment before Annie said, "Yeah, I do need a new outfit."

"I could do with some new clothes myself; I think my mum said there was a sale on at Misfits," Mable chimed in, pleased with the idea.

"Well, that's a date then."

"Why didn't we think of it before?" Annie was glad Wilma thought of going clothes shopping.

"If we catch the early bus, we will be back in plenty of time to get ready to go out," Wilma said. It wasn't long until Annie was singing along to one of the songs on the jukebox.

"Listening to the music is making me feel like going to the Crystal Rooms."

"Yeah, we will be tomorrow, it will make us look forward to it even more," Mable pointed out, trying to reassure Annie.

CHAPTER THIRTY

"It looks like you done a fair few today?" Sid shouted over to Frank.

"Yeah, luckily the machine didn't pack in again. I'm quite chuffed with myself."

"I think your machine has a mind of its own Frank! How you done today, Gilbert?"

"Yeah, I have done more today, perhaps it's because it's Friday."

"Are you going to the Crystal Rooms on Saturday?" Sid asked Frank and Gilbert.

"Yeah, we'll be there. What about you and Suzi?"

"Maybe, depends if Suzi's mum can have the kids."

"What about you Henry, will you be going to the Crystal Rooms on Saturday night?" Frank shouted.

"Maybe later, going to the darts on Saturday with Johnny."

"Blind me! I forgot about the darts on Saturday." Frank was fuming as he had asked Annie out and forgot about the darts match.

Gilbert shouted over to Frank, "I thought the darts was on next Saturday?"

Sid suggested, "Why don't you explain to Annie that you forgot about the darts match and ask if you can meet her later. Who knows she might not mind you taking her to the darts?"

"I will ask her; I hope she will understand the mix up."

"I'm sure she will," Sid reassured him as he collected all the slips each worker had done for the day.

Half an hour before the bell went for home time, Sid asked one of the lads on the factory floor to collect all the parts up on a trolley ready to be shipped out.

By the time Sid finished his job the bell had gone, and everyone was eager to leave.

After clocking out, Frank, Gilbert and Henry went to the café hoping Frank could speak with Annie.

As luck had it, Annie was in the café with Wilma and Mable.

After Frank got his drink, he went over to where Annie was sitting. "Hey how has your day been?"

"Not too bad, met my target which was good." Annie was pleased that Frank had come over to speak with her.

Frank then asked Annie if he could have a quiet word with her. He wasn't sure how to say it, so he just came out with it.

"Well, I asked you out on Saturday and I forgot about the darts which is on Saturday and…"

"I know what you're going to say, can you go to the darts? Am I right?"

"Yes, I thought you might be mad with me." Frank was surprised that Annie was fine with it. "You're right, but I was going to say you can come with me if you like. We can still go to the Crystal Rooms after. I'm sorry, but I did forget."

"I don't mind, honest. What about Gilbert and your cousin are they still coming?"

"Yes, they're still going, I think they will be going to the darts first." After Frank sorted things out with Annie, he shocked her by giving her a kiss on the cheek before he went over to where Gilbert and Henry were standing by the vending machine.

Once Annie had gone over things with Wilma and Mable, Sandra brought over three coffees. "Who are these off."

Sandra said, "They are off Frank and Gilbert." When Annie looked over to where Frank was, they were waving, with big smiles on their face.

"Thank you for the drinks!" Annie said with a big smile on her face also.

CHAPTER THIRTY-ONE

By the time Saturday had come, Sylvia was excited to go to the Crystal Rooms with Bridget. They planned to meet Gregg and Ben in The Running Hare later in the evening.

As Sylvia lay in her bed thinking about Gregg and what a good night it was going to be, she could smell something from downstairs. "I know what that is. Bacon!" Sylvia jumped out of bed then headed downstairs, where she found her mum cooking bacon and eggs.

"Sit down and pour yourself a cup of tea while I finish cooking your breakfast."

"It's no one's birthday, is it?" Sylvia smiled making a snide mark.

"No, I thought we would have a nice, cooked breakfast for a change. Pass me your plate." Sylvia's mum, put the bacon and eggs on Sylvia's plate. Just as Sylvia's mum finished, Sylvia gave her mum a kiss on the cheek. "What's that for?"

"It's for being a great mum." Sylvia's Mum smiled. After Sylvia finished her breakfast, she made her way back up to her bedroom.

When Sylvia finished getting dressed, she thought she would go over the road to see Bridget. With her living opposite Sylvia never had far to go. After knocking on the door, she heard a voice coming from above. It was Bridget at her bedroom window.

"Hey what you doing here? Come on in." Sylvia opened the door and hurried up the stairs to Bridget's bedroom. "So, what time do you want me to be ready for tonight?" Bridget asked, curled up in bed.

"Let's catch the 6.45pm bus then we can go to a few pubs before we meet Gregg and Ben. I hear there are darts on at the Labour Club tonight, so the pubs will be busy." Bridget asked Sylvia if she knew if Johnny was going to the darts? "I'm sure Johnny said he is out with Henry tonight, and he would see us out."

Eventually Bridget got up and dressed then the pair made their way downstairs to the kitchen, where Bridget's mum and dad were sitting drinking tea. Bridget asked her mum, "What's for breakfast?"

"I've done a cooked breakfast this morning, would you like some Sylvia?"

"No thank you Mrs. Molt, I already had mine before I came here."

After Bridget had finished her breakfast, she and Sylvia decided to go to the park. As Sylvia and Bridget walked along the park Sylvia had an idea. "I never thought 'til now, I bet Gregg and Ben would like to see the darts. That's if they like darts."

Bridget told Sylvia, "They can do whatever they want, as long as we go to the Crystal Rooms. I'm not sure what to wear tonight, with all those bargains we got last week from 'Misfits.'"

"Let's wear one of the swing dresses we bought," Sylvia suggested feeling delighted with herself for suggesting it. "I will wear the cream one with flowers on the rim."

"Yeah! And I will wear the blue and white one." Bridget was also excited about meeting Ben and wearing a new dress on her date.

After Sylvia and Bridget had been walking a while, Sylvia suggested they sit on the bench and watch the children playing ball games. It was a lovely, sunny day and there were many folks out walking their dogs or sat on the grass sunbathing. It wasn't long until Sylvia and Bridget started talking about the murders. "Still can't believe Vera was murdered. Who would do such a terrible thing?"

Bridget went on, "Let's just hope they catch the killer soon it's making me feel on edge all the time".

After Sylvia and Bridget sat watching the children play, they both thought they should start walking back home to start getting ready to go out.

CHAPTER THIRTY-TWO

While Annie was getting ready to go on her date with Frank, she started to feel nervous, although excited at the same time. She'd had a good time out shopping with Wilma and Mable. They had bought some lovely clothes in 'Misfits' sale.

Annie was taking ages to choose what outfit to wear, but eventually picked a swing dress - dark blue with flowers on it. She had also bought cream shoes which would go with the dress. It was perfect for her date with Frank, even though they were going to the darts first.

Annie had bought some Babycham to calm her nerves down. By 6.45pm she was more than ready to meet Frank. She was wondering how Wilma and Mable were feeling if they were as nervous as she was for their date.

When it was 6.55pm Annie left her flat to go and catch the bus on the corner road, which was only a few minutes' walk. When Annie was on the bus, she was feeling butterflies in her tummy. Annie was trying to focus and not letting her nerves spoil her date. When the bus finally got to the stop it was 7.25pm - there was five minutes spare.

Annie had only been waiting a few minutes when she could see Frank coming in the distance. He was dressed in his fine clothes with his black hair slicked back. "Hey, you look gorgeous!" Annie went red in the face. Both were feeling nervous. Even though they worked together, being on a date was different somehow. "So where would you like to go first?" Frank asked.

"Well, I thought we could go to The Running Hare."

"Yeah, sounds like a plan to me." Annie could see Frank didn't know what to say as they made their way to The Running Hare she thought she would try breaking the ice.

"So, will Gilbert and your cousin, Billy be up the Crystal Rooms later?"

"Yeah, I think they are feeling nervous about meeting the girls. Although I think they said they will go to the darts first."

"They won't change their minds, will they?" Annie asked, feeling concerned.

"Oh no, they both want to meet them. They're just... you know?" Annie knew what Frank meant to say.

As Annie and Frank reached The Running Hare it was still light out, but the pub had already started to get busy. When they eventually reached the bar, Frank asked, "What would you like to drink, Annie?"

"A Gin and Tonic, please." After they got their

drinks, Annie noticed Sid and Suzi in the corner by the window. Most of the workers of All Parts were out on a Saturday night.

"Hey, what you two doing here?" Frank liked to joke with Sid and Suzi.

"Same thing as you two I expect," Sid joked back. "So, is this for keeps then?" Sid teased Frank and Annie.

"Hey Sid, leave them alone will ya?" Suzi knew it must be their first date. "Come sit with us? Long as you two don't want some privacy?" Suzi smiled.

"No, we will sit by you two." Annie was glad in a way, as it might be better someone was with them. Suzi then asked Annie if this was their first date, as she hadn't heard about it yet.

"Are you sure you want me and Sid with you on your first date?"

Annie smiled and spoke, "We'd rather you were with us, I think. I definitely feel more relaxed with you two with us."

CHAPTER THIRTY-THREE

By the time Sylvia and Bridget got on the bus, it was already 7 o'clock and they were meeting Gregg and Ben in The Old Hag at half past. They were both starting to get nervous as it was only their second date.

"Hurry up Sylvia else we will be late!" Bridget was feeling a bit up tight, as they had plenty of time to get to the pub with ten minutes to spare.

When Sylvia and Bridget arrived at The Old Hag it was busy with not many seats left. As Sylvia ordered their drinks, Bridget went to sit down making sure to keep some seats for Gregg and Ben.

Just as Sylvia got the drinks and sat down, Gregg and Ben walked in.

Sylvia and Bridget were pleased to see them after a long week. When Gregg and Ben got their drinks, they went to sit down with the girls. It wasn't long until Sylvia started talking about the darts and asked Gregg if he knew about it.

"Well, me and Ben were just talking to a bloke in

The Old Slipper he was saying most of the folk will go down there as it was a late bar."

Sylvia glanced at Bridget then at Gregg. "Would you two rather go to the darts?"

Gregg was surprised Sylvia asked. "If you two don't mind going, we would like to go."

Bridget gave a faint smile then agreed. "Darts it is, as long as we go up the Crystal Rooms later."

After finishing their drinks, all four went to the Labour Club to see the darts. The darts had already started, so the main room was already quite busy. When Gregg and Ben went to get the drinks, Sylvia and Bridget eventually found somewhere to sit. Once they were sat down, they waited for Gregg and Ben to come over with the drinks.

Gregg made it obvious that he and Ben wanted to go over to where they were playing darts. Sylvia and Bridget never really understood what all the fuss was about with the darts. One, it was crowded. Two you couldn't really see the darts match. It seemed a lot of work to watch it.

"Would you two mind if we went to a couple of pubs then meet you up the Crystal Rooms?" Sylvia glanced at Gregg then Bridget waiting for an answer.

Gregg nodded. "Long as you two don't mind us watching the darts."

Sylvia and Bridget just laughed. "No, we don't mind at all. So, we will see you up the Crystal Rooms." Gregg got up to give Sylvia a kiss on the cheek then Sylvia and Bridget went.

CHAPTER THIRTY-FOUR

When Johnny left his digs, it had just turned 7 o'clock. He hurried to catch the bus on the corner of his road. Within two minutes the bus turned up. Johnny jumped on and headed straight to the back of the bus.

When the bus reached his stop, he lit a cigarette as he jumped off then walked the rest of the way to The Running Hare to meet up with Henry.

When he got to The Running Hare it was quite busy. Johnny wrestled to get to the bar but couldn't see if Henry was already in the pub or not. After getting his pint of lager, he stood by the bar and lit another cigarette.

Not long after Henry came into the pub, saw Johnny standing at the bar and made his way over.

"Hey, you're late aren't ya?" Johnny teased Henry.

"Nah, I inner, my watch says 7:30pm." After glancing at their watches, they both laughed.

"We will have one here, then go and see the darts. Is that alright with you?" Johnny asked. Henry agreed.

After finishing their drinks, they made their way to the Labour Club. By the time Johnny and Henry arrived, it was that packed that most of the folk were drinking outside. Even though it was that busy Johnny and Henry got to the bar and were served quite quickly because everyone was busy watching the darts.

After they both got their drinks, they tried to see if they could get nearer the darts match, but they could only see the heads of the people who were playing. Johnny could see Frank and Gilbert watching. It was all right for them as they were at the front.

Henry turned to speak to Johnny. "Let's get out of here, we can't see anything. We should have come here first. I never thought it'd be this busy though." Johnny agreed and they both necked their drinks back. "Shall we go back to The Running Hare?"

"Yeah, no good here, we could have a game in there?"

"Yeah, sounds like a plan to me." Henry nodded in agreement.

CHAPTER THIRTY-FIVE

All through the day Wilma and Mable had been looking forward to going to the Crystal Rooms. Even more so because they were meeting Gilbert and Billy up there. Wilma and Mable had both picked out new dresses to wear - Wilma had a light blue swing dress and Mable picked the darker blue - they both looked stunning. Before they left the house, they both had a Gin and Tonic.

Soon as it was 6.45pm they hurried to catch the bus on the corner of their street. With them both living in the same street it was easier for them to meet up. Just before 7 o'clock the bus arrived and, as they got on the bus Wilma almost missed a step which started them off laughing.

"One of these days you're going to break a foot!"

"Well, it's these heels, they are deadly to walk in," Wilma moaned while rubbing her ankle. On the bus, both girls were in a happy mood, wondering which pub to go in first. "I think we should go in The Running

Hare first. As it should be quiet with the darts on." When they reached their stop, they walked the rest of the way to the pub.

To their surprise it was busy, they could hardly get to the bar and, when they did, Mable suggested to have double Gin and Tonics being as it was packed.

At the bar Wilma said, "At least we haven't got work tomorrow, so I suppose it won't hurt us having doubles." Wilma whispered to Mable "I wonder how Annie is getting on with Frank? I bet they are in the Labour Club, watching the darts?"

By now Wilma and Mable were quite tipsy. After lighting a cigarette Wilma noticed a table free, so they both marched over to sit down, but Wilma missed the seat and fell on the floor which got them both in a fit of laughter. Suddenly this fine gentleman came over to help Wilma up on her seat.

Just then Annie and Frank came into the pub. Annie couldn't believe they were so tipsy. While Frank, went to the bar to get their drinks, Annie stayed talking to Wilma and Mable.

"How many drinks have you two had?"

"Well, we have been drinking doubles to save us keep going up to the bar." Mable whispered to Annie.

"Just take it steady you two, you haven't even got up the Crystal Rooms yet?"

"Don't worry about us, we will be all right, you'll, see?" Wilma then went up to the bar to get more drinks. Annie knew they wouldn't listen, they never did.

"Gilbert and Billy are still in the Labour Club, they said they will see you two ladies up the Crystal Rooms a bit later." Frank told Mable, she just smiled. Frank whispered to Annie "They are merry, aren't they?"

"They are always the same, they will slow up when they get to the Crystal Rooms."

"I was getting worried I would have to help carry them home." Frank joked to Annie.

"I hope it doesn't come to that!" Annie gave Mable a strange look. At the bar, Wilma was still talking to the man who helped Wilma up off the floor.

"How was the darts?" Mable asked.

"Fair play, there was some good dart players, we enjoyed it didn't we Annie?"

"Yes, to my surprise I enjoyed it, different." Annie grinned.

After they all finished their drinks, they decided to have another drink in The Running Hare as Wilma was still talking to the stranger. Just as Frank got a round in, Sid and Suzi came back in.

"Hey, did you enjoy the darts?"

"Yeah, there was some good players this time, better than last year," Sid said whilst getting the drinks in.

"Come sit with us?" Frank asked.

"You sure, you're not fed up with your misses already?" Sid, joked. They all laughed.

"No, never." Frank looked at Annie, then he gave her a peck on the lips.

"Arr true love, is it?" Sid teasing again.

CHAPTER THIRTY-SIX

Sylvia looked at her watch, then said to Bridget, "Shall we go to The Old Slipper else we won't have time?"

"Yes, let's go now," Bridget said before knocking back the rest of her Gin and Tonic.

By the time they both got to The Old Slipper it was so packed out that it took a while to get to the bar.

While Sylvia and Bridget were ordering their drinks, Johnny and Henry came over to where they were. "I wondered when I would bump into my girls."

Sylvia could see that Johnny and Henry were quite tipsy. They were both glad they bumped into Johnny as he was always up for a fun night.

"Where are your dates?" Johnny asked.

"Oh, they were at the darts." Bridget filled Johnny in. "We are meeting them up the Crystal Rooms in a while."

"How you keeping Henry, did you enjoy the darts?" Sylvia asked him as he swayed slightly, smiling a little too widely.

"Yes, really enjoyed it."

"We will walk up with you two ladies to the Crystal Rooms. Be safer with us, babe." Johnny was always looking out for Sylvia and Bridget, even more since the murders.

"Yes, I think we will. Our knight in shining armour, aren't you Johnny?"

"Yes, I am indeed." Sylvia and Bridget laughed. "Shall we have one more then go?" Everyone agreed and sent Henry off to get some more drinks.

By now the pub was not so packed, with many of the folk going up to the Crystal Rooms. Sylvia and Bridget went to sit on chairs by the window.

Johnny was talking to Henry about the match between Manchester United and Arsenal on the 26th of April. Everyone was going.

"That is all Johnny has been going on about this last month, is football. Everyone reckons it's going to be a good match," Sylvia said to Bridget. "Gregg has asked if I like football and would I like to go with him on the 26th? I said I would. What about Ben, has he asked you?"

"I told Ben I would go but I am not too keen on football, so I'm not sure if he got a ticket for me. Well, I think we should be going up the Crystal Rooms, else we won't get any seats. I'm not sitting on those stools by the bar, they're so uncomfortable to sit on!" Bridget complained.

"I reckon men are worse than women for chatting. We will never get them away from here." Sylvia shouted for them to hurry up with their drinks.

Then, a few minutes later, they were all ready to go to the Crystal Rooms.

CHAPTER THIRTY-SEVEN

After Frank and Sid got more drinks in, they went back to sit with Annie and Mable. It was not long until Frank and Sid got talking about the football, which was the following Saturday. Frank, Henry, Gilbert and Sid had bought tickets to go and watch them live. With the match between Liverpool a few weeks back, Manchester looked to be on good form.

"I've been waiting for this match for weeks now. I wouldn't miss it for anything," Sid said to the others. Suzi was also going to the match. "When we go anywhere, we go together, as it stops all the rows. The missus can't have ago at me if she's there too. It makes sense. That is free advice for you, Frank." Frank laughed then glanced at Annie.

By now, Wilma had finished talking to the man who helped her up, when she fell off the stool.

"You been talking to that man for a long time." Mable was not happy Wilma had left her to talk to a stranger.

"Sorry, but I couldn't be rude when he helped me up off the floor, now could I? And he bought me a Gin and Tonic which was nice of him." Wilma was now trying to wind Mable up. "His name's George, thanks for asking! And he said he would buy me a drink up the Crystal Rooms."

"Have you gone mad; you're supposed to be meeting Gilbert up the Crystal rooms?"

"I don't think Gilbert will mind George buying me a drink."

Annie shook her head in disbelief, she could not understand how Wilma couldn't see what she had done. "Well, we can't do anything about it now," Annie said, trying to make sense of it all.

"Shall us girls have another drink before we go up the Crystal Rooms?" Mable suggested while drinking the last bit of her Gin and Tonic.

"Why not!" Wilma agreed, whilst putting her hand out for Mable's glass.

"Just because you're buying me a drink doesn't mean I forgive you." Mable gave her a snarky look.

After everyone had drunk their drinks, they were ready to go to the Crystal Rooms. It was only just up the road which meant they didn't have to go too far. As soon as Wilma walked into the large room, her eyes looked around the room. "Yes, there's a table over there in the corner."

"Let's hurry before someone nabs it!" Wilma was like a soldier on a mission as she grabbed Mable's hand and powered forward towards the empty table "Mable, I think it is your turn to buy the drinks next."

"Yes, it is. Gin and Tonic?"

"Yes, get me a double, then I will get you a double when it is my turn."

While Mable was getting the drinks, Gilbert and Billy came in the room. They headed straight to the bar where Frank and Sid were with Annie and Suzi. "I will go and sit with Wilma and Mable if that's alright with you?" Annie whispered to Frank.

Frank then whispered back to her, "I don't mind, long as you're happy with it?" He bought her a Gin and Tonic, then kissed her on the lips. Annie knew the lads would only be talking about football.

CHAPTER THIRTY-EIGHT

By the time Johnny, Henry, Sylvia and Bridget got up to the Crystal Rooms it was already crowded. Sylvia and Bridget could not see if Gregg and Ben were up there or not so they went up to the bar with Johnny.

After Johnny got the drinks in, Sylvia and Bridget stayed at the bar, as by now there wasn't any tables left. Johnny went to talk to the other lads at the bar.

"I can see Gregg and Ben, They're over the other side of the bar." Bridget said starting to wave to get their attention. As soon as Gregg and Ben saw Sylvia and Bridget, they went over to them.

"How long have you been up here?" Bridget asked Ben.

"Only about fifteen minutes," Ben replied.

"We'll have to stand or sit on the bar stools, but they are uncomfortable!" Sylvia moaned.

"Never mind we can dance instead." Bridget, as always, trying to look on the bright side. Gregg gave Sylvia a kiss on the lips and put his arm around her to comfort her. Sylvia smiled and leaned her head on his shoulder she was happy just being in Greggs arms. Not long after, Johnny came over. Sylvia introduced Johnny to Gregg.

"Hey, nice to meet you." Johnny shook Ben's hand, and it wasn't long until Johnny, Gregg and Ben were talking about the football.

While Johnny was talking to Gregg and Ben, Bridget pulled on Sylvia's arm to come and dance as one of Bridget's favorite songs had started playing. "Come on, my song will be finished else?" They were in good spirits dancing and singing to their favorite songs. By now the room had gotten more crowded with more people coming on the dance floor.

When Sylvia and Bridget went back from the dance floor, Gregg asked Sylvia if she wanted another drink.

"Yes, I'll have a Gin and Tonic please. I will go and get them if you like."

"If you don't mind, babe?"

Gregg offered to pay for the drinks, but Sylvia said, "No, it's my turn to buy you a round." Sylvia also asked Johnny, Ben and Bridget if they would like a drink.

"I'll come and help you," Bridget said as she linked her arm with Sylvia's and they headed for the bar.

CHAPTER THIRTY-NINE

After Annie, Wilma and Mable got more drinks in, Wilma noticed George over the other side of the bar. He was looking over to where Wilma was sitting with Annie and Mable.

"Wilma don't look at him else he will come over." Annie was concerned George would cause trouble between Gilbert and Wilma.

"Come on, let's have a dance," Mable suggested, trying to change the subject.

As Annie, Wilma and Mable were dancing, they could see George staring the whole time.

When they'd had enough of dancing, they went to sit back down and Wilma told everyone, "I will get the next round in, Mable will you come with me to get the drinks?" Mable nodded that she would.

Annie went over to speak with Frank who was on the other side of the bar talking with Johnny, Henry, Gilbert and Billy. "I thought Gilbert and Billy was going to speak with Wilma and Mable?" Annie was starting to feel aggravated about Gilbert and Billy messing Wilma and Mable about as they hadn't gone over to talk to them all night.

"I think they will, I did mention it to them." Frank was clearly not sure what to say to Annie. She knew Wilma and Mable wouldn't be messed about by men.

When Wilma and Mable got the drinks in, they went back over to their table. As soon as they sat back down, Annie saw George go over to talk to Wilma. Annie hurried over to speak to her. "What are you doing?"

"Well at least George is interested in me. Not like Gilbert."

Annie didn't blame her - she was right, so she let it be.

Wilma had been talking to George for a while and she'd learned that George was in property - he owned a fair amount in fact. She found herself enjoying his company and, after a short while, George asked Wilma if she would like a dance. She said yes straight away and the two made their way to the crowded dance floor.

Then, out of the blue, Billy came over to speak to Mable and asked if she would like a drink. "I will have a Gin and Tonic, please." Although he'd taken his time Mable was glad that Billy had eventually come over to speak to her.

When Wilma and George sat down, Gilbert came bustling up behind George and hit him. Of course, this started a fight with many punches flying between Gilbert and George.

Suddenly Johnny came over to try to split them up. "Stop. It's not worth fighting." It was no use, the two men were too much for Johnny to keep apart, so Frank had to pull Gilbert away.

Wilma went to George to take care of his bloody nose, giving him her handkerchief to stop the bleeding. Gilbert went back to stand by the bar with the other lads and Johnny went back to his pint.

"It could have been much worse if Johnny hadn't come to split them up," Annie said, impressed Johnny had managed to split them up so fast.

Frank got Annie another Gin and Tonic before the bar closed then Frank asked Annie to dance with him. Annie was surprised she didn't have Frank pegged as a dancer. Frank put his arms around Annie like he was never letting her go again.

At least Annie had the last hour with Frank, they were getting along so well. She glanced at Mable and, to her surprise, saw her sitting at the table kissing Billy. Wilma was talking to George, and he was telling her that she was worth the fight. Wilma then leaned her head on his shoulder.

After Gilbert finished his drink, he left the room and went home. Leaving just Henry and Johnny to finish their pints. Soon after the dance ended, the main lights came on and everyone started to leave and go home.

CHAPTER FORTY

The next morning Sylvia woke up early. She was on a high after the great night she'd had with Gregg. Sunday, she had a lie in, but when Sylvia opened the curtains, she could see it was a lovely sunny day. She started thinking about Bridget and Ben she thought how lucky they both were to find two lovely blokes.

Now she was awake Sylvia decided to get up and have her breakfast then, later, go and see Bridget. As Sylvia was walking down the stairs, she could hear her dad talking to her Uncle Mack.

"You're up early for a Sunday," Sylvia's mum said while she cooked breakfast. "So, what would you like for breakfast?"

Sylvia just stared then spoke, "Bacon and eggs please, Mum. Oh, and a cup of tea."

"I see in the paper they have no more leads on the two murders," Sylvia's Dad said to Mack. Then asked her, "I hope your new fella walked you home last night?"

"Yes, he did, Dad." Sylvia knew her Dad was only

keeping an eye on her. Her Uncle Mack was her dad's brother, he lived on the outskirts of Manchester.

"They want to catch whoever killed those two, before they strike again!" Sylvia's dad said. Sylvia almost forgot about the killings for a while. Her mind was on Gregg.

After Sylvia had eaten her breakfast and gotten dressed, she went over the road to Bridget's house. Just like before, she knocked on the door, Bridget shouted from her bedroom window, to come up. When Sylvia got to Bridget's bedroom, she'd just finished getting dressed.

"We had a good night last night, didn't we?" Bridget said while she was brushing her teeth.

"Yeah, we sure did."

"With Johnny helping to stop the fight, he's practically a hero." Sylvia and Bridget burst out laughing.

"So, are you still coming to watch the match on Saturday?" Sylvia asked.

"Yes, I will be. Gregg told me he has got me a ticket. He can get tickets easy as his uncle is their sports therapist."

"I do know Bridget: it was Gregg's uncle who got ours."

"Oh right, I forgot you would already knew about Gregg's uncle."

"Let's not tell many people else they will be asking us to get them tickets. Gregg might not like that. You see what I mean?"

"No, I completely understand," Bridget quickly

answered. "I'm rather looking forward in going to see Manchester United play live."

Sylvia stayed at Bridget's house a while then she went back home to have her dinner with her Mum and Dad. After she'd eaten, she went up to her room and read some more of Jane Eyre, not long after, she fell asleep with the book on her chest.

CHAPTER FORTY-ONE

The Inspector was waiting on the news of the fingerprints on the batteries in the torch, he was hoping luck would come his way - he needed a break.

A call came through from the lab, but the news wasn't what the Inspector was hoping for. There was only a partial fingerprint on the batteries; not enough to find the killer.

The Inspector knew the killer had to be found before there was another murder. Even the blood type wasn't enough to stand up in court. With two murders, the Inspector was hoping for a break in finding the killer. The Inspector had a feeling someone must have seen something, either Mr Dent's murder at the factory or Miss Jones' in the park. If someone did see something, were they too scared to come forward?

The Inspector had to think hard where to go next. Either interview the workers again or just sit back and wait for something to happen, but the Chief Inspector was putting pressure on to solve the case.

He knew he had to catch the killer soon, it was a race against time. Whatever he decided, there was just one thing. The killer was dangerous, whoever it was.

CHAPTER FORTY-TWO

By Monday, the factory workers were raring to do a hard day's work after the enjoyable weekend they'd had. Frank, Henry and Gilbert were in full swing. "I'm really looking forward to the match on Saturday," Frank said to Sid.

"Yeah, I haven't been to watch Man United since last season," Sid went on to say, whilst checking the parts coming through.

"Man United have done well this season, I reckon they will beat Arsenal easy." Frank said to Sid.

"Forget United, the rate you're going, you will beat your last best," Sid gushed. "So, you and Annie are an item now then?"

"I think you know the answer to that, Sid."

"Annie is a lovely girl." Frank just smiled, then carried on working. "Gilbert is it true that I heard a girl blew you off the other night?" Sid waited for a reply, but Gilbert just carried on working, not saying a word. "So, I take it, it's true then?" Sid left it there. Frank looked at the time and there was only half hour until lunch time, so everyone just got on with their work.

Annie, Mable and Wilma had been working hard all morning, but it wasn't long until the conversation turned to Mable and her new bloke. "How did you get on with Billy Saturday night?"

"Well Billy walked me home and that was it."

"So, you won't be going to the football match?" Annie quizzed.

"No, you know I don't like football. I'd sooner go round the pubs, than watch football," Mable moaned.

"You're quiet Wilma?" Annie trying to get Wilma talking but she knew what Annie was like.-"You're not going to be like this all day, are you?" Annie was like a dog with a bone: there was no way she was stopping until Wilma started to talk

Then, "No I'm not. Just not going to talk about Saturday night."

"You do know what I want you to talk about!" Wilma didn't reply. "All I want to know is if you are seeing George again?"

"Well, the answer is no and I'm not saying no more! Me and Mable are going out on Saturday."

"So, what about you, are you meeting Frank?" asked Mable.

"I'm meeting him later. So, if it's alright with you two, can I come out with you both Saturday night?"

"Oh, I don't know, what do you think Mable?" Annie went quiet. "What you think, do you really have to ask?" Wilma grinned then the three girls laughed loudly.

CHAPTER FORTY-THREE

When Sylvia and Bridget were doing their work, Johnny whispered to them.

"Your blokes are sound. I was talking to them for a while on Saturday night."

"Yes, they are. We noticed you were talking with them half the night!" Sylvia and Bridget just burst out laughing.

"What's wrong?" Johnny was surprised they laughed.

"It's nothing. We're glad you got on with Gregg and Ben."

"Oh, is that their names?" Johnny asked. They all laughed.

Their replacement supervisor heard and told them to be quiet and get on with their work.

"At least he isn't worse than Brian," Sylvia spoke quietly to Bridget and Johnny.

Johnny then wanted to know, "Are you two going to the match on Saturday?"

"Yes, we are going to the match as Gregg's uncle works at the club. He's a sport therapist for Man United, so managed to get us some tickets."

"Blimey, that's handy for getting tickets!" Johnny was surprised.

"Yes, it is, but keep it under your hat," Sylvia whispered.

"Got it," Johnny replied.

"It's you next?" Sylvia told Johnny.

"What you mean, me next?" Johnny looked puzzled by the question.

"Find a nice girl for you."

"You don't need to worry about me," Johnny blushed.

"Yes, we do. Then it will be a six sum."

"Good luck to you, no one would want me!"

Sylvia was shocked Johnny said that. "My dad says there is always someone out there for you. It's not just my dad who believes that I do as well." Sylvia had to make a point.

"Sometimes I forget about the two murders, now the police aren't coming here anymore. It is like it never happened," Bridget mumbled as she looked in the filing cabinet.

"I don't think they have a clue who done it!" Johnny said, while pointing to his watch. It was near break time. A few minutes later the bell went for lunch.

As soon as everyone had eaten their lunch it was not long until the bell went to go back to work.

When Sylvia, Bridget and Johnny got back to the office, they were in a good mood.

After their meal in the canteen, they knew they could just sit back and chat as they had done most of the work in the morning and the supervisor was out for the rest of the day.

CHAPTER FORTY-FOUR

As usual there was a queue to get into the canteen. Once Sid got his meal, he went to sit in his usual seat. It was always busy in the canteen on a Monday as it was a roast dinner and treacle pudding.

"What's the news on the murders? It has been a bit quiet this last week," Frank asked whilst stirring his cup of tea.

"Yes, it has been quiet since the police stopped coming to the factory." Sid nodded in agreement.

"At least we will have a good day at the match on Saturday," Henry said, trying to change the subject.

"Yeah, it will be a good one. We deserve it with everything going on around us," Sid said. Gilbert and Henry agreed. "It has been a while since I've been to watch a live match. With the three kids, we don't have the time, so it be nice to watch the football, just me and Suzi. To be honest, I think Suzi is looking forward to going just as much as me."

"Well at least she enjoys your company Sid, most

girls wouldn't want to see a football match," Henry teased.

"Yeah, I must agree Suzi isn't a bad lass. I love her for it," Sid said as he went along.

"I'm counting down the days till we go to the match," Henry admitted.

After lunch, Frank was about to start back to work, when his machine packed in. "That's great! I will never be able to do my days quarter now." Frank wasn't happy.

"I'll put you on Pete's machine. He was owed a half day, so he's gone home. His machine is exactly the same as yours, so you shouldn't have any problems with it."

"Good job, else I would have been in trouble, Sid."

"Yeah, it did work out well."

It wasn't long until Frank was up to speed and Sid came back to tell him that his machine was going to be fixed that afternoon and it'd be ready for him the next morning.

CHAPTER FORTY-FIVE

Inspector Wright thought he would get all the PCs involved in the murder case so he could go over both murders with everyone to refresh their minds.

"Today we will be going over both murders. Mr Brian Dent was found murdered at a factory *All Parts* on April 4th around 2.30am. The victim was dressed in a brown jumper, black trousers and brown shoes.

Mr Bill Mills told us the last he checked on the offices was a round 12 o'clock and the office was empty and locked. Then at 2.30am he found Mr Dent lying face down on the floor near the desk. So, Mr Dent was killed between midnight and 2.30am.

There were also signs of a struggle, as there were chairs tipped over and the desk had been left a mess. The killer must have taken Mr Dent's key, as his wasn't on his body nor has it been found in the office. Also, the windows were locked. Next to Mr Dent's body was a rubber glove, and a torch, but no murder weapon left at the scene.

There was a considerable amount of blood coming from the victim indicating he was murdered where the body was found. The murderer must have come through the door and left that way. There was in fact someone running away from the factory, seen by Mr Bill Mills, but he couldn't see who it was as it was too dark. At least one of the workers, must know something. It is a matter of waiting till one of them cracks.

With the partial fingerprint not being enough to convict, as the fingerprints we took of the factory workers weren't conclusive to the partial fingerprint. A major blow, I know, but we should not give up just yet!

Now, with Miss Vera Jones, she was found on the 13th of April in Heaton Park by a dog walker at roughly 3.30am. She was dressed in red jumper and navy-blue trousers, brown shoes and a long, dark brown coat. Miss Jones was last seen at bingo around 10.15pm. She had one stab wound in the back of the neck, then three blows to the head. With the amount of blood at the scene, suggests she was killed then dragged behind the bush where she was found.

As in the case of Mr Dent, there was no murder weapon found. There was a cinema ticket found by the body with a spot of blood - B positive - on the corner. Maybe belonging to the murderer, as the victim was A positive. I have a feeling the cinema ticket holds the key, to cracking this case.

Now Man United will be playing Arsenal this Saturday, it will be busy in Manchester especially the pubs. I want you to be extra vigilant, there will be extra policing on that day.

If you see anything suspicious do not hesitate to ask for assistance."

After the briefing the Inspector sat at his desk, you see he had a good idea who the murder was, but he hadn't enough evidence to arrest the person, not yet anyway...

CHAPTER FORTY-SIX

Just before the bell went for home time, Sylvia asked Johnny, "Are you coming to the café with me and Bridget, after work?"

"Yes, I could do with a coffee right now." No sooner had Johnny said yes the bell went. Everyone was more than ready to leave. When Sylvia, Bridget and Johnny went into the café it was quiet, only a few people were in there. Sylvia agreed, she would get the coffees in.

"Any news on the murders?" Sandra asked while making the coffees.

"No news but I suppose the police know what they're doing," Sylvia quickly responded by not letting on too much to Sandra.

Sandra never said another word after that. She just got on with making the coffees. "Could you also do a few rounds of toast as well?" Sylvia asked then thanked her when she nodded.

"You can sit down, and I will bring everything over to your table." Sandra gave an awkward smile.

Once Sylvia sat Bridget said, "I'll put some music on while we wait for our drinks," then got up and waltzed over to the jukebox.

Not long after, Sid, Frank, Henry and Gilbert entered into the café. "Hope you're putting something good on?" Sid said whilst winking at Bridget.

"Oh yes, I will just for you, Sid," Bridget sarcastically replied. By the time Bridget finished putting music on, Sandra had brought the order over to their table. "Blimey, toast as well? We are being spoiled," Bridget said while taking a bite out of her piece of toast.

You should be thankful for what you get," Sylvia gave a look at Bridget.

"I was only joking; you are touchy today." Sylvia never said anything else on the matter.

"I hope we enjoy the football match on Saturday. As it will be a long day if we don't."

Bridget gave a sigh, as she lit a cigarette. "Yeah, I hope so too, but I have a feeling we will enjoy it. If we don't, we will know not to go again. We can meet them after the match when they go next time."

As usual Sid was on the vendor machine while Frank, Henry and Gilbert were messing about. To his surprise, Sid won the jackpot again. "Trust you to win the jackpot, I was going to have a go after you." Frank was gutted.

"You'll know next time, to come on here before me, won't you?"

"Yeah, maybe I will."

CHAPTER FORTY-SEVEN

The next morning the birds were singing, and it was another lovely day.

Annie was up early, and she couldn't help but think how nice it would be to spend a day in the garden instead of having to go to work in a stuffy factory all day. But she could not afford to have any time off work; she needed every penny that she earned.

After getting dressed and eating breakfast it was 7.15am and she was ready to go and catch the bus. Just as she reached the end of the road the bus turned up; it was early this morning.

When Annie got on the bus, she thanked the driver for waiting. Wilma and Mable were already sitting down on the bus as they lived a few streets away from Annie, slightly closer to the bus stop.

"You made it then," Mable said whilst lighting a cigarette.

"Yeah, I did, but the bus is early this morning! I just hope the rest of the week goes by smoothly."

"I can't wait till Friday; I can see this week is going to drag on."

"Don't think about it and then you won't notice it," Annie said, trying to make sense of it all. Wilma had been quiet since the Crystal Rooms when George and Gilbert had their fight, but Annie knew Wilma enough that she would say if something was wrong.

Just then the bus reached their stop right outside the factory. After Annie, Wilma and Mable clocked in, they went straight to their line of work and started packing parts, idly chatting about what they got up to at the weekend.

CHAPTER FORTY-EIGHT

In the office, Sylvia was looking through some old files in Brian's old office. Mr Mortimer had asked her to sort it all out that morning.

"It's going to take me forever to get through all this crap"

"Just throw it in the bin, no one will know!" Johnny advised Sylvia.

"Yeah, it'll be my luck the Manager finds out."

"I could help you if you'd like?" Johnny suggested.

"No, I will go through it after I've done my work and clear through it this afternoon. I'll do another hour then start on the wage slips." Sylvia carefully went through each piece of paper, which was mostly invoices for different metals the company bought in to make the parts.

Just as Sylvia was going through the last pile of files, she came across a folder. Something made her look at one of the sheets of paper. When she read it, it had a list of names Sylvia knew from the factory. In fact, it was the same list as the Inspector had but this list had the reasons why Brian was black mailing them.

Sylvia was shocked and couldn't believe what she saw on the list. She quickly put it in her pocket, so no one would see it, but now she was worried as to what else she may come across. Sylvia knew the Inspector would love to get his hands on that list, but Sylvia wasn't sure what to do with it. Should she throw it away or hand it in to the Inspector?

Before Sylvia knew it, the bell went for lunch time. "Are you going to look through that all day?" Bridget joked to Sylvia.

"No, I'm coming now." Bridget wondered what was up with Sylvia as she was acting strange. "I need to go to the toilet," Sylvia shouted to Bridget. When she went in the toilet, she looked at the list again. She couldn't believe what she saw, she was stunned. One name stood out on the list. Not sure what to do, she put the list in her handbag then went to have lunch with Bridget and Johnny.

"You seem quiet, you alright?" Bridget sounded concerned.

"Yeah, I'm fine I think I just needed some food and a drink; I feel much better now." Sylvia thought it better to say that. After they ate their lunch, all three went to have a cigarette outside the back of the factory before they went back to the office.

CHAPTER FORTY-NINE

When Frank, Henry, Gilbert and Sid got back from lunch, Frank was raring to go and to beat his best. Even though Frank was always the one who could do the most, he always set a target for himself to beat.

"I'm going to beat you one day, Frank!" Gilbert shouted over to him.

"Yeah, you can try!" Frank replied.

But Gilbert and Henry knew they could not beat Frank, even though they tried every week.

Just as Frank finished his last part, the bell went for home time. Frank wanted to get home early as he had boxing with Gilbert and Henry so, instead of going to the café, they caught the bus home.

Luckily all three lived close to each other on a housing estate in the middle of Manchester. When it reached their stop, Gilbert said, "We will be round yours at 6 o'clock," as he and Henry walked away from Frank.

Every day when Frank got home, he would have a game of football with his two younger brothers. Then, when it was teatime, he would sit with his dad and talk about the time when he was in the army in the first world war. Frank liked to hear his dad's stories while having his tea.

"You off boxing tonight?" Frank's Dad asked, even though his dad knew he was.

"Yeah Dad, I'm off in a bit."

"I wish I were your age again, my lad. I used to do a bit of boxing when I was your age."

Frank smiled even though he'd heard it all before.

Not long after Frank had finished his tea, he went up to the bathroom to get washed and changed before he went boxing. As soon as he was ready, there was a knock on the door. When Frank opened the front door Henry and Gilbert were stood there. Frank shouted to his mum in the garden that he was off and he'd see her later.

The place where they boxed was not far from their house. There were two boxing rings, one with two other lads using it and the other was booked for Frank, Henry and Gilbert who usually went boxing on a Tuesday and a Thursday.

Once they got changed into their gear, Frank and another lad started boxing, while Gilbert and Henry practiced on the punching bags.

Gilbert lived with his mum, dad and a younger brother and sister. Henry also was still at home with his mum and dad and two younger sisters. All three had been best friends since primary school. Now they were 21, they always looked out for each other or helped if they were in any trouble.

There were two middle aged ex-boxers who ran the

boxing ring - Jeff and Graham - who would keep the boxers in check and decide the winner.

Frank, Henry and Gilbert had been boxing since they were twelve years old, so all three were good.

"Bloody hell, Frank, will I ever win against you?" The other lad, Dave, said after the first match was over.

"Maybe next time, Dave."

When it was time for Gilbert to box, there was another lad called Reece wanting to challenge him.

Half an hour later, Gilbert had beaten Reece and it was the same for Henry. The other lads hadn't been boxing long, in a way they looked up to Frank, Henry and Gilbert.

After the three men had finished their boxing and gotten changed, they went to a local pub: The Falling Star. They had a few beers to unwind.

As it was a Tuesday, the pub wasn't too crowded, just a few elderly men out for a quiet pint who would talk to Frank, Henry and Gilbert about how they were getting on with the boxing.

"You taking Annie to the Football on Saturday?" Henry asked.

"No, I don't think Annie likes football that much. I am meeting her after in The Running Hare. Why'd you ask?"

"Oh, just wondered how Mable got on with your cousin?"

"I see. I don't think he is seeing her again; I don't think Mable liked him in that way."

"I thought I might ask Mable out," said Henry.

"Mable is a pretty lass," Frank thought out loud.

"I will ask her out either at work or on Saturday," Henry told Frank.

CHAPTER FIFTY

The next few days went by slowly for Sylvia; she still wasn't sure what to do with the letter. She had been on edge since she found the list and was in two minds what to do with it. So, she decided to hide the letter in her room, a place no one could find it until she could decide what to do with it. She pushed all thoughts of it away and concentrated on looking forward to going to the football with Gregg. As Sylvia glanced at the clock, she saw that there wasn't long until the bell went for home time. Sylvia asked Bridget and Johnny if they were going to the café after work.

"Nothing will stop me going to the café, I could do with a coffee," Johnny replied. Johnny would say the same thing every time he was asked to go to the café.

"Me too, can't wait to get out of here," Bridget whispered, as the new supervisor was in today.

When the bell went Sylvia, Bridget and Johnny couldn't get out of the office quick enough. After they clocked out, they headed straight for the cafe.

"I'm so glad it is Friday tomorrow," Bridget said feeling relieved it was nearly the weekend.

It was Johnny's turn to get the coffees in this time. "I want three coffees thank you."

While Johnny was waiting for the drinks, Sandra was asking him all sorts of questions. Sylvia and Bridget could hear Sandra flirting with Johnny.

"That woman makes me feel sick," Bridget moaned as she filed a nail which had broken when she was at work.

"I guess you are going to the football match on Saturday?" Sandra asked as she made the drinks.

"Yes, I will be going. Will you be there?" Johnny asked trying to be friendly.

"I'm not into any sports." Johnny didn't say anything after that. He just took the coffees and went to sit with Sylvia and Bridget.

"We could hear that Sandra flirting with you." Bridget had never liked Sandra, she always thought she was cheap.

"I never noticed," Johnny shrugged, then winked at Bridget. Bridget rolled her eyes and took a sip of coffee.

"So, who are you going with to the football match?" she asked to change the subject.

"I'm going with Frank, Henry and Gilbert," Johnny replied. "I'm really looking forward to it"

"We might see you there then?" Bridget smiled, then turned to Sylvia.

"You're quiet today?" Bridget wondered.

"I've just got a bit of a headache, that's all." Sylvia didn't want to tell them the real reason.

Sylvia had a feeling that she wouldn't be able to sort this out on her own.

CHAPTER FIFTY-ONE

At last, it was Saturday morning and Sylvia was excited to go to the football with Gregg. Thank, God it wasn't raining - it would have been terrible to stand in the wet for 90 minutes.

She was up early because she could hear someone in the kitchen and when she went to investigate, she found her mum cooking breakfast.

"Morning darling, would you like a fried breakfast this morning?"

"Mum, you're up early. I think you're making a habit of it."

"Oh, I was a wake so I thought I would make breakfast as you're going to a football match. You'll need something warm inside you."

"Aww that's sweet, Mum. So… do you know what time the match starts?"

"Sylvia! I thought you would have known that, or at least Johnny or Gregg would have told you? Well, it's 3 o'clock."

"Mum, I knew that, I thought it was a special match and it would start earlier."

"Now you mention it you've got me wondering now!" Then Sylvia and her mum started laughing. "What time will you be meeting Gregg today?"

"I think he said to meet in The Running Hare at 1.15pm. Bridget is calling for me at 12.30pm and we're catching the 12.45pm bus into town."

"Just be careful. The police still haven't caught the killer yet."

"I will do, Mum."

As Sylvia's mum went into the garden to hang the washing out, Sylvia was left on her own to think about the letter she had hidden in her bedroom. The thought kept going over what she should do.

In a strange way she was feeling guilty going to the football match.

Just then Sylvia's mum came back in from outside. "I think I can hear your dad getting up. I'm going to make another cuppa would you like one?"

"Oh yes, I wouldn't say no, Mum."

"I better fry some more bacon for your dad too."

When Sylvia's dad was up, he reached straight for the morning paper. "I see there's no news about the murders. I thought the police would have caught him by now!"

"What if it's a woman?" Sylvia's mum replied.

"Or a woman. Clever Clogs." Sylvia's dad gave a strange look. "I bet the police haven't a clue who did it. Have the police been at the factory this week?" he asked Sylvia.

"No, they haven't, I think the whole factory is wondering the same, Dad."

"I would say the tea has brewed by now." As Sylvia was pouring the tea her dad started to eat his breakfast. It wasn't long until he started asking Sylvia about the football match.

"So, this is the first time you have been to a live match?"

"Yes, it might be my last as well!" All three laughed.

"Trust you to say that, Sylvia." Her mum shook her head.

After drinking her tea, Sylvia went back up to her bedroom to get washed and changed, ready for when Bridget called.

When Sylvia was ready, she lay on her bed thinking about the letter and what she should do about it. She couldn't even tell her mum and dad, if she did that it would make it real. She thought she would get the football out of the way first, then she could decide what to do.

Sylvia couldn't understand how the letter got into Brian's invoices - it was too sinister to be found in the work files. It was stupid of Brian to leave it around. Whatever happened, Sylvia was going to enjoy the football match with Gregg and friends.

A short time after, there was a knock on the door. Sylvia then gathered her things and went downstairs to answer it. It was Bridget calling for her. Sylvia shouted to her mum that she was leaving.

"Have a good time!" Sylvia's mum shouted back.

As Sylvia and Bridget walked to the bus, she tried to

forget about the letter. But she couldn't help thinking she should have handed it into the police. She or someone else could be in danger. if the killer ever found out she had something to help capture them.

But she wasn't thinking straight, she only wanted to have some fun.

When the bus arrived, Sylvia and Bridget went to sit at the back. After they both lit a cigarette, Bridget could see that Sylvia was not herself.

"Is everything alright with you?" Bridget was concerned. It'd had been a while now that Sylvia had been a lot quieter than usual. "We are going to have fun today!" she said, trying to cheer her up.

"Yes, we are! Take no notice of me, I've just been having these headaches." Once again Sylvia was trying to hide the real reason.

When they reached their stop, they walked the short distance to The Running Hare.

"I will buy the first drinks, are you having a Gin and Tonic?" Bridget asked Sylvia.

"Yes, please."

They both decided to sit at the bar, as it was starting to get busy. Bridget could tell whatever was bothering her friend was more than a headache, but Bridget knew Sylvia too well - she would tell her in her own time.

By now the pub was packed as most folk would go in The Running Hare before they went to the match or listened on the radio.

Not long after, Gregg and Ben came in.

"You just timed that right, as my glass is empty." Bridget laughed as she tried to wind Gregg and Ben up.

"Well, mine's a larger then," Ben teased Bridget.

"I was only joking, Ben."

"Well, I thought you were asking?"

"He's got you there, Bridget," Sylvia chimed in, trying to make a point. Then all four burst out laughing.

CHAPTER FIFTY-TWO

After Frank had finished his breakfast, he went to play football with his kid brothers. With it being a fine day, it kept them out of mischief while their mum did the chores.

"Thank you, Frank, I love it when you're here, as they play me up rotten!" Frank's Mum said while hanging the washing out on the line.

As usual, Frank's dad was in his armchair reading the morning paper.

When his mum finished her chores, Frank went to get ready to meet Henry and Gilbert.

"I'm off now, Mum!" Frank shouted as he left the house.

A few streets away were Henry and Gilbert's houses. Frank knocked on Henry's front door and waited for someone to answer as Gilbert walked up behind him.

"Hey mate, you ready for the game?" Frank asked.

"Yeah! Can't wait to go!" Henry opened the door, shouted goodbye to his parents and all three then made their way to The Running Hare for a few pints before the match.

When they got there, it was packed with supporters waiting to go and watch the match. After a wait at the bar, they got their drinks. All three abandoned the idea of finding a table and stayed at the bar. In the corner of the room was Sid and Suzi. Soon after, Johnny came in.

"Not long now!" Johnny said while taking a sip of his beer.

"We'll have a few beers then we're off."

By now it was 2pm and Frank and the others were keen to make a move.

CHAPTER FIFTY-THREE

As Annie sat in her small garden, she wondered how Frank was getting on at the football. She told Frank she would meet him in The Running Hare after going out with Wilma and Mable. She told Wilma and Mable to catch the 3.45pm bus, so they could have some time together before she saw Frank.

After Annie came in from the garden, she took a bath then got ready to meet the girls.

By the time Annie was ready it was 3.30pm, she needed to hurry or else she would miss the bus. She only had a few minutes to catch it. As usual, Annie had to hurry to get there on time. Luckily, she had a minute to spare before the bus came. When she got on, she could see Wilma and Mable waving at the back. "You were lucky you caught it this time," Mable said.

"Yeah, I didn't think I was going to." Annie was feeling relieved.

"I bet you're looking forward to seeing Frank later?" Wilma asked.

"I am. I haven't seen him much this week." Annie sighed. "Well, there is one thing I know and that is we are going to enjoy ourselves tonight," Annie reassured Wilma and Mable.

As soon as the bus got to their stop they got off and made their way to The Running Hare. By now the pub was packed with folk listening to the football on the radio.

"I will get this round in," Wilma said as she waved a note in the air. "Three Gin and Tonics, please," she told the bar man.

As soon as all three got their drinks, they went to sit down by the window. Annie could see Wilma was in a better mood and thought now would be the Time to ask her about George. "How are you getting on with George?"

Wilma didn't answer straight away. "I'm not seeing him again. It just didn't work out that's all." Annie did not push her anymore.

"Whatever happens we are going to have some fun and not worry about men."

"I can't argue with that!" Mable agreed wanting the same as Wilma.

CHAPTER FIFTY-FOUR

As Sylvia, Gregg, Bridget and Ben went through the gates, they made their way to the stands. Sylvia and Bridget were surprised by how many people were there, it was quite a sight.

After Gregg and Ben got refreshments, the game was about to start. The whistle went and within the first ten minutes Rowley had scored for Man United.

A short while into the game Sylvia and Bridget were starting to enjoy themselves. They were surprised by just how much.

The time was going by so fast. Rowley had scored two more times, making it 3 - 0.

"What a good game!" Ben said to Gregg.

"I bet you're glad you came?" Gregg whispered to Sylvia.

"Yes, I am. Thank you," Sylvia replied then gently kissed Gregg on the lips.

When it was half time Sylvia and Bridget went to the toilet while Gregg and Ben went to get more drinks.

While Sylvia was in the toilet, she was still thinking about the letter and whether she might be able to talk to Gregg about it.

"How long are you going to be?" Bridget was eager to get back to Ben.

"I'm coming now! What's the hurry?" Sylvia came out and washed her hands.

"I'm really enjoying the game, are you?"

"Yes, I am. It's a great game." Sylvia was trying to be happy but there was so much on her mind to think about.

When they got back to Gregg and Ben, the second half had already started. "We haven't missed much, have we?" Bridget asked sounding disappointed.

"No, it just started, babe," Ben reassured her. After five minutes Arsenal scored their first goal and the atmosphere was buzzing. There was nothing to worry about as five minutes later, United had another goal. All the fans were cheering by now, it was a sight to see.

"I bet you will want to come again?" Sylvia smiled then nodded her head, agreeing with Gregg.

With the last half hour to go things were intense: Man United had missed two more opportunities. All the fans were singing their teams anthem, hoping it would encourage the players to score another goal. It nearly worked for Arsenal as one of their players nearly scored a brilliant goal, but Man United got the ball again and scored another goal. It looked like Man United were going to take the cup.

With all the cheering, it was hard for Sylvia to hear what Bridget was saying.

With only five minutes to go, Byrne took the ball and scored his first goal for United. Then the ref blew his whistle, and the crowd went crazy.

CHAPTER FIFTY-FIVE

After Frank, Henry, Gilbert and Johnny had a few more pints, they made their way to the stadium. By now there were hundreds of folks going to watch the game. They were so excited!

After they showed their tickets, they all headed to the bar to get themselves a drink. While at the bar they bumped into Sid and Suzi.

"Why don't you two come and watch the game with us?" Frank asked while waiting for his pint.

Once everyone got their drinks, they headed to watch the game. Luck had it, the game hadn't started yet. With the ref's whistle, the game began. After ten minutes there was a cheer as Man United scored a goal 1-0. With Suzi being short, she had a job seeing the game, but she did't mind, she just liked spending time with Sid. With so many misses from Man United, it kept their fans on edge.

"What a game. Come on!" Frank shouted. With only ten minutes to half time, Man United scored yet again.

All the fans were cheering, and Frank and the others could not keep their eyes off the match. There was only five minutes to half time now.

"They're playing well," Sid said to Frank.

Only two minutes to go before half time. Just when they thought they wouldn't score again, there was a massive cheer as Man United scored once again. Frank, Henry, Gilbert and Johnny jumped up for joy, then the referee blew his whistle for half time. Frank and the others were laughing and singing, as they went to get more drinks at the bar.

After talking a short while Johnny said, "Man United are playing really good, can't wait to see the other half." Henry and Gilbert agreed with Johnny.

"We better get back to where we were. They'll be back out soon," Frank told the others. No sooner as they got back to where they were before, the players came out.

The ref blew his whistle, and the game was back on. After five minutes play, Arsenal scored their first goal making it 3 - 1. By now the fans on both sides were singing away, it was a great atmosphere.

Then fifteen minutes into the game Man United scored once again and Sid and Suzi were jumping for joy, as were the others. Everyone was in good spirits; it was a great game.

At full time the whistle went the crowd started cheering again. Frank and Johnny were jumping up for joy.

Frank shouted, "3 - 1."

CHAPTER FIFTY-SIX

Everyone in The Running Hare was listening to the radio and were cheering for Man United. Annie knew then that Frank would have enjoyed the match, with the score being 6 - 1. Wilma and Mable were chatting to folk in the pub as usual. Annie wasn't sure what time Frank and the others were coming into The Running Hare.

"I'll get the next round in," Mable said as she collected the glasses off Annie and Wilma. Eventually Mable got to the bar. "I'll have three Gin and Tonics, please."

While Mable was waiting for the drinks, Frank, Henry, Gilbert and Johnny came into the pub. They headed straight to the bar.

"Would you like a Gin and Tonic?" Frank shouted over to Annie.

"Yes, please." Even though Mable was getting more drinks, Annie didn't say anything to Frank, as she was in good spirits with Man united winning the cup.

When everyone got their drinks, they all went to sit with Annie, Wilma and Mable. Wilma was blushing and feeling a bit awkward when she saw Gilbert. "Sorry about last week at the Crystal Rooms," Wilma whispered to Gilbert.

"That's alright, water under the bridge."

After Wilma broke the ice with Gilbert, they couldn't stop talking to each other. It was the same for Henry and Mable - they both were getting on so well. They were all talking about the match and how well Man United played. By now Sid and Suzi had joined them.

CHAPTER FIFTY-SEVEN

After the match, Sylvia, Gregg, Ben and Bridget made their way downtown to the pubs. All the folk in the streets were singing and in a cheerful mood. The first pub they went in was The Old Hag. It was really busy with all the fans celebrating Man United winning the league - it was a night to remember for many years to come.

Once they found a table, they sat down. Gregg and Ben could not stop talking about the match, they were still on a high.

Now the match had finished and there was nothing to distract her, Sylvia started thinking about the letter. Bridget knew there was something wrong, as Sylvia was so quiet. Bridget thought if she got some Gin and Tonics down her, she might tell her what was wrong. "Right, I think we should celebrate Man United winning today!" Bridget thought that would be a good excuse to drink, so she would get doubles for her and Sylvia.

"We'll drink to that," Gregg and Ben held their glasses up.

"I will get the next drinks in," Bridget insisted. When she went up to the bar, she was thinking that she hadn't ever seen Sylvia so quiet. The last was when Brian molested her in the office. Bridget wondered what had upset her so much. When Bridget went back with the drinks, she said to Sylvia "I wonder how Johnny got on with the lads?"

Sylvia just gave a faint smile, whatever was bothering her, she was bottling it up. It was that bad it was a wonder Gregg didn't notice it. Then suddenly Sylvia spoke, "It is my turn to buy the next round. Shall we go to The Running Hare next?"

Bridget looked surprised. Gregg and Ben agreed to go to another pub.

"We could come back here after, if you want to Sylvia?" Gregg said trying to please her.

"No that's fine, let's go to another pub." Sylvia gave Gregg a kiss on the cheek. When they got to The Running Hare it was even more packed than the last pub. There were a lot of folks from the factory that must have been to the match.

When Sylvia was at the bar getting the drinks, she could see Johnny with the other lads, in the corner of the room. It sounded as if they were getting merry with all the cheering they were doing.

By now Bridget had seen Johnny too. "Hey there stranger," she said then gave Johnny a kiss on the cheek.

"So, what did you think of the match?" Johnny asked.

"Yes, we all enjoyed it. We will definitely be going again!"

"That's good." Johnny went on to ask Bridget "What's up with Sylvia?"

"I'm not sure, she has been like this a few days now. I thought I'd get a few drinks down her to cheer her up, but it doesn't seem to be working." Bridget was feeling defeated. "Are you going up the Crystal Rooms?"

"We might be, will see what the others want to do first."

"Well, if you do, I will see you up there." Johnny said.

"I better get back to the others," Bridget said and went back to her seat. "Johnny says hi," she told Sylvia. "Shall we go up the Crystal Rooms?" Bridget was eager to go."

"If you want, we'll go." Ben smiled. If Bridget really knew the reason why Sylvia was so quiet, she would understand why.

CHAPTER FIFTY-EIGHT

"I'll get this round, Frank. I haven't bought one yet."
Annie pulled out her purse. Frank told Annie to put her
money away. "I insist!"

Frank wouldn't hear of it.

"Oh well, don't say I didn't offer." Annie smiled.

By now Sid and Suzi had joined the table. Johnny
leant over to whisper in Sid's ear "Have you got
anymore parts for me to sell down London?"

"I'm not doing that anymore. It's gotten too risky. If
I get caught, I will lose my job. Or worse, I might end
up in prison, I told you that before." Johnny wasn't
happy with that, he thought he would have come round
now the police had stopped coming to the factory.
"Anyhow don't you earn enough working at the factory?
You're on your own, with no wife or kids to support.
Whatever do you do with your money?"

Johnny never answered - he could see Sid wasn't
going to change his mind. After lighting a cigarette,
Johnny went to sit back down with the others. "Are we

all up for going to the Crystals Rooms? At least it's a late drink up there," Frank asked everyone, though he already knew Annie wanted to go.

"Shall we have one more drink than we can go?" When they'd all finished their drinks, they were quite tipsy by that point. After leaving the pub, they made their way up to the Crystal Rooms determined to make a night of it.

Once in the Crystal Rooms they all headed straight to the bar. With it being busy, it took them a while to get served. "We are never going to get a table, that means we will have to stand all night. Even the stools are taken!" Mable was feeling sorry for herself.

"It doesn't matter you can sit on my leg if you want to?" Henry said to Mable.

Mable gave Henry a strange look, then told him. "I don't think so." Henry laughed. "I was joking."

Now Wilma and Gilbert were starting to get on she'd completely forgotten about George. She was soon reminded when she saw him on the other side of the bar. "Oh no!" Wilma told Gilbert. "It's that George!"

"If he bothers you so help me, he's in for it," Gilbert shouted angrily while giving George a strange look.

"When he walked me home last week, I felt like I was being interrogated! Asking me all these questions about the murders, it was creepy." By now Gilbert, Henry and Johnny were intrigued wondering what George was up to.

"What did he ask you?" Gilbert asked Wilma.

"It was weird, like he was a policeman or a reporter. Asking if I was close to Brian and Vera. I told him I was on packing, and I didn't know them that well. He asked me to go on a date with him, but I said I didn't want a boyfriend at the moment."

"Oh, I see, so you don't want me then?" Gilbert teased.

"I just said that to him to get rid of him." Then Wilma realised Gilbert was teasing her.

"I bet he's a copper," Johnny said, trying to figure out if George was in fact one.

"Well, he told me he was in property."

"He would say that. He wasn't going to tell you he was a copper, he was just nosing around," Gilbert said. Wilma was feeling a bit of a fool, not knowing if George was a copper.

"They do that a lot, pretend they're someone else so they can find things out," Johnny told Wilma.

"I'll remember that in the future." Wilma lit a cigarette then glanced at Gilbert, then they both burst out laughing.

CHAPTER FIFTY-NINE

When Sylvia, Gregg, Ben and Bridget finally went up to the Crystal Rooms there were no seats.

At the bar, Sylvia was getting the next drinks in with Bridget when they saw Johnny at the bar.

"I hope you're in a better mood than you were in The Running Hare?" Johnny was waiting for Sylvia to answer, but Sylvia just gave a faint smile. "Perhaps I spoke too soon," Johnny laughed hoping Sylvia would too, but she didn't.

Not long after, Gregg noticed Sylvia was crying. "Whatever is a matter?" Sylvia just told him she had a bit of a headache. "Maybe you should stop drinking if you have a headache?" Gregg was concerned.

"Yeah, maybe you're right."

Sylvia's head was all over the place, wondering what to do. She wished she had someone to talk to about the letter, keeping it to herself was torture and the loud music wasn't helping.

When Sylvia went to the toilet, Johnny went to asked

Gregg, "What's up with her, she's been quiet these last few days?"

"I think she's been having these headaches. Could you go and check on her, she has gone to the ladies?" Gregg turned to Bridget, worried about Sylvia.

"Yes, of course I will."

("From now on, everything is about to change! In the next few hours to come, Inspector Wright will be on the trail to catching the killer. Will the Inspector get the killer in time? Or will someone else be in danger? If you haven't guessed who the killer is by now, this is the time to do so!")

When Bridget got to the ladies' room, Sylvia was sitting on a chair. "Whatever is a matter?" Bridget was concerned for Sylvia by now.

"I found something at work, a letter!" Bridget was confused as to what Sylvia was talking about, so she pushed for more information. "It's something Brian had in his office. You know the invoices Mr. Mortimer asked me to sort out? You see, this one piece of paper... well, it wasn't to do with the factory, but what Brian had written down."

"So, what did it say? Tell me Sylvia, you're scaring me?" Bridget by now could see it was something serious. "Well?"

Just as Sylvia was about to tell Bridget, Annie came in.

"Whatever is a matter? You look dreadful!" Annie asked.

"She's just got a headache!" Bridget said quickly.

"I would get home and get to bed if I was you," Annie suggested trying to help.

After Annie had gone Bridget turned back to Sylvia. "Now tell me what's wrong."

"Well on the paper is a list of names. When I first saw it, I thought it was for over time, something like that. Then I looked closer, opposite the names were prices, then reasons, it is sick. It is a list that Brian had. He'd been black mailing the workers and who he was going to black mail."

"How do you know the ones he was going to black mail?"

"Because on the list was Johnny's name, it said, Johnny was a Nazi Officer, and he was a killer!"

"What? No. How did Brian find out that?"

"Who knows!"

With her hand on her mouth, Bridget's face went pale, she was in shock!

"You know what this means?" Sylvia went on.

"What?" Bridget was eager for Sylvia's answer.

"It means Johnny is the killer. I know he is! Think about it?"

Bridget went quiet. "He can't be." Bridget couldn't believe what she was hearing.

"I don't know what to do with the letter. All this time we were friends with a murderer."

"But he is our best friend, how could he have done those murders?" Bridget was in denial. "If we take it to the police, they will arrest Johnny!"

But Sylvia and Bridget knew deep down what they should do. "A Nazi Officer. He couldn't be, not all those Jews that were murdered. How could he?" Bridget was horrified.

"All these years we have known him, who would have thought." Sylvia and Bridget were shaking and crying, it was all too much to take in at once.

"I've just had a thought… what will he do to us if he finds out we know?" Sylvia's face went white as a sheet with the thought.

"We can't let him find out we know?" Sylvia goes on to say to Bridget. "We will clean our faces and sort our make-up, then tell Gregg and Ben that we have to leave as I have a headache. Gregg already thinks that's what's wrong with me. Then go to my place, pick up the letter and take it to the police station."

"Let's do it!" Bridget agreed.

So, the first thing they did was check their makeup. Then hurried back out to where Gregg and Ben were standing.

"We thought you left us?" Gregg teased Sylvia.

"I think it has been a long day, that's why I have a headache. Would you mind if we go home?" Sylvia asked as she leaned her head on Gregg's shoulder.

"That's it, let's get you home." Gregg said before finishing his beer. After saying goodbye to the others, they made their way out of the Crystal Rooms. "I will call for a taxi, you girls can't walk all that way with a headache."

Sylvia thought it was nice of Gregg to think of her. Before the taxi came Sylvia whispered to Bridget. "I think it's better we tell Gregg and Ben now before they hear about it in the papers?" Bridget thought for a moment, then agreed with Sylvia.

"We have something to tell you two." After Sylvia

and Bridget told Gregg and Ben everything, they were shocked.

The two men stepped forward and hugged each of the girls. "You've known this for days. You poor thing, no wonder you're not feeling well. Carrying that information around with you," Gregg comforted her.

By the time the taxi arrived, Sylvia was beat. "Let's get you home." In the car, Gregg put his arms around Sylvia then kissed her on the lips tenderly. "Do you want us to come with you to the police station?"

"Yes, I want you all with me if you don't mind?" When the taxi reached Sylvia's house, she ran upstairs to get the letter she'd hidden the day before. Luckily, Sylvia's parents were in bed asleep.

Not wasting another minute, they headed straight to the police station. When they got there, they asked to speak with Inspector Wright. "When will he be back?" Sylvia asked after being told he wasn't in.

"There's been a development in the case, not sure when he will be back," PC Green said." Sylvia had an idea to go and wait for Johnny to get home.

"I don't think that is a good idea!" Gregg says to Sylvia.

CHAPTER SIXTY

At the police station a call came through for Inspector Wright. It was Mr West - Vera Jones' brother-in-law. He needed to speak with the Inspector.

"Inspector, will it be possible for me to come to the station? I need to speak with you, it may be something to do with this case."

"Oh, I see. Yes, come in. I will be waiting for you." The Inspector was intrigued to what Mr. West wanted to talk to him about.

As Miss Jones' house wasn't that far away from the police station, Mr West got there in about ten minutes. When he arrived, PC Lamb showed Mr West into Inspector Wright's office. "Please take a seat Mr. West. So, what can I do for you?"

"Well, I'm not really sure there is something."

"Please go on, it must be something, else you wouldn't have come. If it is the smallest thing tell me." The Inspector could see Mr West wanted to get something off his chest.

"I'm not really sure if it is anything to do with this case or not. Oh well, here goes. A couple of years ago, my mate Bobby Bentley was murdered when he was at work in a grocery store."

"Wait a minute, I know this case, it was when I was in London, we never caught the killer." The Inspector couldn't believe it, maybe there was a connection after all.

"You see, before he was murdered, he was in the RAF. I know, a big difference from the RAF to working in a grocery store in Peckham. But Bobby liked working there, with his injury to his leg he wasn't able to do much else. Well, he had this photo from the second world war. Don't ask me where he got it, he wouldn't tell me. I often asked him, but he would always say 'If I told you, I would have to kill you!' I always thought he was joking, but now I'm not so sure he was.

Something did tell me he'd gotten it from a mate who was a prison of war in Germany. I think his name was Gerald Spencer, he was also in the RAF. I believe he got captured in 1943 when his plane came down when he was bombing Germany. Anyway, he had a photo, and, in this photo, there were Officers, German Nazi's. Bobby did tell me that these Nazi Officers were pure evil. They were the ones who ordered all those poor Jews to be murdered in those camps, in Poland and Germany.

I feel bad I never told anyone before, but when Bobby got murdered I was scared they would come after me. You see, not all the Nazi Officers got caught and hanged. Some escaped Germany and came over here or anywhere with different I.D." By now the Inspector could not believe what he was hearing.

What I can gather is, this one day Bobby either saw this Officer in the shop or somewhere like that. Bobby must have approached him - which turned out to be a terrible mistake. I admit Inspector, Bobby did tell me when he saw this Officer, but he spoke perfect English. He swore to me it was one of those Officers in the photo he had. I know I should have come forward, but I was too scared at the time. Not just for me, but my family.

I wasn't sure if the Officer was a customer or someone who worked in the grocery store. Not 'til I came up to Manchester to stay with my wife's sister. It was the weekend when Vera was murdered. I thought I would give my wife and Vera some time together. Which, they both went to a picnic, Vera's work organised it.

I went to a few pubs, seeing as Man United were playing Liverpool thought I'd try and catch it on the radio. I was enjoying listening to the football then I went in The Running Hare. That is when I saw a face I couldn't forget; it was the German Nazi Officer. All places I would see him, it was here in Manchester. But to be honest I had seen him before in London, a pub called The Wild Fox. As I knew his name after, I did a bit of digging. His name was Carsten Fischer, he was born in England, he had German parents - that's why he speaks perfect English. His parents went back to Germany just before the war. He had a good up bringing, spoke English, German and French - that's how he became an Officer; his parents were well off.

You see, Inspector, I do have the photo. I received a large letter in the post years back. When I opened it, it was the same photo Bobby showed me weeks before. I was so scared I nearly ripped the photo up and threw it in the fire. I couldn't understand why Bobby had sent the photo to me until he was killed a few days later. Luckily, I had changed my mind and kept it under the floorboards. These last two years I've been worried sick in case the killer of Bobby realised I had been sent the photo and they came looking for it.

"I couldn't live with myself knowing all this, especially after Vera was killed. It was too much of a coincidence to ignore anymore. I don't want anyone else to get hurt. He's evil. If he suspects anything, he won't hesitate to kill you. I gather he goes by Johnny Hill now."

As soon as the Inspector heard that name, he knew he had gotten the right man. He knew he had to act fast before he killed someone else. The Inspector wasn't fooled by his charm, though that is how Johnny Hill has been getting away with it all this time. The Inspector had a strong feeling it was him.

As soon as he'd slipped up on his alibi the night Miss Jones was murdered. Johnny had told the Inspector that he left the bingo hall before it started at 7.30pm, but Sid Holmes told the Inspector he and his wife Suzi, saw Johnny leaving the bingo hall after 10pm. Also, he had been to the cinema at the Majestic that same afternoon. His cinema ticket was found with a stain of blood, at the murder scene of Miss Jones. And when Brian Dent was murdered, Mr Henry Davidson had seen Johnny arguing with Brian Dent at the back of the factory the day before.

The only thing the Inspector didn't have was hard evidence and he thought the motive for the killings was black mail. He never dreamt the killer would be a Nazi officer that had escaped Germany but, in the end, the Inspector knew he would catch a break.

"Mr West, if you could get that photo to me, it would be strong evidence against Mr. Hill?"

"Yes, I will get the photo to you as soon as I can."

Not wasting another minute, the Inspector made his move by taking his men to look for Johnny Hill. It was a race against time!

CHAPTER SIXTY-ONE

As Sylvia, Gregg, Bridget and Ben got back into the taxi, Sylvia gave the taxi driver Johnny's address. When they got there, Gregg warned Sylvia not to confront him, just to wait and see if the police were there waiting. If they weren't then they'd know the police didn't know it was Johnny.

When the taxi got to Johnny's flat, it was in darkness. After Gregg and Ben paid for the taxi, they stayed. Luckily, there was a bench close by.

"Should we leave this to the police?" Bridget was unsure about getting too involved.

"Let's wait another ten minutes then we will go," Sylvia convinced them, but then in the dark, there was a figure walking. It was Johnny.

Sylvia couldn't keep it in anymore and ran straight up to him. "It was you all a long!"

Johnny just laughed. "Whatever are you on about?" Johnny looked puzzled as to why Sylvia was there.

"Was it you who murdered Brian and Vera?" Johnny

did not answer, he just walked on. "Why won't you answer me?"

Then Johnny asked, "What are you asking me that for. Are you joking?"

"No, I'm being serious!"

"I guess you're not alone?"

"No, I'm not, Gregg, Ben and Bridget are with me."

"I gathered that. You and Bridget can come up to my flat, but no one else."

Sylvia hurried over to Gregg and told him Johnny's conditions. "As soon as me and Bridget go up to his flat, call the police. He won't do anything to us."

Gregg was concerned, "Are you sure?" Sylvia nodded so, reluctantly, Gregg and Ben both agreed. Sylvia and Bridget then followed Johnny up to his flat.

When they entered, he asked them to sit on his sofa. "Drink?" Johnny asked as he lit a cigarette.

"No, we don't want a drink, we want answers?" Sylvia told him without losing eye contact.

"Where shall I begin?"

"At the beginning!" Bridget replied.

It was the first time Sylvia and Bridget had seen inside Johnny's flat. The room itself was small, more like a bed sit. The front room was quite dark with only a lamp in the corner of the room. Bridget and Sylvia were expecting something much bigger and glamorous than a small room like this.

"Why did you kill Brian and Vera?" Bridget thought it better to keep him talking.

"You see, now I am confused! I didn't kill Brian, but I did kill Vera!"

"Wait, what? You didn't kill Brian?"

"I've wanted to - on many occasions. To sort that low life out. Blackmailing me, who did he think he was?! But someone else beat me to it. They did me a favour to be fair."

"Why was he blackmailing you?"

"He found out something about me. Something I'd hoped would stay a secret so I could forget about it. I don't know how, but he said something about he heard me talking to someone in German. Then he did some digging. He knew there was more to me than meets the eye."

"Come on, there's more to it than that?"

"What a clever girl, Bridget. There is more to it."

"At least tell us the truth. You owe us that. We've been friends with you all this time." Sylvia couldn't believe someone could do the things he had done.

"Well, I suppose it won't hurt telling you now. To start with, my real name is Carsten Fischer and in fact I was a Nazi Officer. Even though I was born in England, my parents moved back to their homeland - Germany - when I was ten years old. That was in 1931. As you know I speak fluent English. I became a German Officer in 1942, when I was 21.

I suppose me speaking English, French, German and my family having money helped me become an Officer so young. Also, my father had connections with other wealthy families.

I know you are judging me and yes, I did some bad things when I was in Germany. You've got to see my point of view - I had my orders. I flew from Germany in

1944, when I could see we were going to lose the war. When I had all my I.D, I left Germany on a French fishing boat. With me speaking French, I got away easily. Everything was going fine, 'til someone had a photograph of me in my uniform. They recognised me where I worked. I was a supervisor in a small grocery shop in the east end of London, two years ago."

Sylvia and Bridget couldn't believe what he was saying, they were so shocked. These last two years since they had known him. How he could sit there and tell them all this evilness he was saying?

"I thought I was in the clear till Vera kept on."

"How did Vera work it all out?" Sylvia asked Johnny.

"Not sure how she found out, but I was quite surprised when she told me. She wanted me to hand myself in. Also, God would forgive me and all that crap. She gave me two days to do it."

"Was that the reason Vera wanted to speak with you that Friday before the picnic?"

"Yes, it was. Sylvia well done you remembered. You could imagine how shocked I was when she told me? She said, 'Do the right thing.' Well, I couldn't have that now, could I? Sad really, how she put the ball in my court, so to speak. I didn't mind Vera."

"It never really got you far, did it? Now we know who you are?"

"I suppose you want us killed now?" Bridget realised what she had said.

"Now you mention it, I will have to wont I?" It went quiet for a moment.

Then Sylvia remembered, "What about your parents, where are they now?"

Johnny then spoke softly. "They were both killed in the war, by a shell bomb, it hit my parents' house, in 1943. I was surprised you worked it all out Sylvia."

"Well, I didn't know you killed all those Jews in Germany and Poland?" Sylvia still couldn't believe Johnny could have done all those evil things.

"So, you didn't have any brothers or sisters?" Sylvia pushed for more information. "I'm glad you asked that question. It happens that I did have a younger brother and sister. Their names were Mila and Friedrich. Sadly, they also got killed in the bombing."

"So how old were they? When were they killed?" Sylvia asked bluntly.

"Mila was twelve and Friedrich would have been Fourteen. I know you think of me differently now you know everything, but you must see my point of view. If only Vera had minded her own business." Johnny was starting to get irritable as he lit another cigarette.

As soon as Johnny told her that, Sylvia could feel her temper start to boil. "You cannot justify what you've done. You killed all those innocent people. You had a choice not to do it, but you did it anyway. Why didn't you leave Germany before you were ordered to kill those people?"

Johnny did not speak straight away, just stared. "Maybe I should have, but I was made to believe it was the right thing to do. It wasn't just me who was ordered to kill those Jews. There were other officers that were much worse than I was. Besides, they would have killed me if I disobeyed their orders."

Was Johnny a born killer? Or was he brain washed to do all those terrible things? Whatever it was, it did not change the fact that he committed murder!

"Well now you know everything, I suppose you're going to the police?"

"You leave us no choice; we have to do the right thing." Sylvia and Bridget were feeling nervous.

There was another thing Bridget wanted to ask Johnny. "When you were friends with us these last two years, was that real?"

Johnny thought for a moment then said, "Yes, that is the sad bit. I really thought a lot of you. You two were my best friends."

A tear dropped from Bridget's eye thinking of the good times she'd had with Johnny.

"I know you and Bridget will do the right thing; I wouldn't expect anything different."

Suddenly Johnny noticed a light flashing from outside his window, there were three police cars waiting. "I see you have already been to the police?" Sylvia didn't respond. "Can I ask you one question?" Sylvia and Bridget wondered what Johnny wanted to ask them. "How did you find out it was me who killed Vera?"

"A few days ago, when I was at work Mr Mortimer asked me to sort out Brian's paperwork in his office. When I was going through it, I came across a list of names. People Brian was black mailing. On the list was your name, opposite your name it said why he was black mailing you. It said you were a Nazi Officer who escaped from Germany. I then assumed it was you who did both of the murders."

There was a knock on the door. "Well, we know who that will be?" Johnny said quietly.

"Come out with me and Bridget, you know it is the right thing to do now," said Sylvia.

Johnny was reluctant to go but, lighting a final cigarette, he went with them.

Once Sylvia, Bridget and Johnny were outside, three policemen came to put him in handcuffs. They took him straight to the police station to be questioned. Inspector Wright stayed to speak with Sylvia and Bridget. The Inspector looked at them both. "I know how you both feel, someone you care for hiding all that evilness. Not knowing what they were up to behind your back."

Sylvia spoke to the Inspector first, "I have some evidence I found in Mr Dent's belongings. I found it a few days ago in his office." She gave the letter to the Inspector and said, "Johnny said he didn't kill Brian Dent. Only Vera. I thought you should know, even though I'm sure Johnny will tell you in his interview."

"Thank you, Miss Weston. I'm sure what's in there will be particularly good evidence against Mr Hill. I know it has been a shock for you and Miss Molt, to find out your friend has done horrendous things. I will need to question you both tomorrow at the police station. Say... midday?"

"Yes, that will be fine for us." Sylvia felt like it was someone else who was talking to the Inspector.

"Will you be coming together?" The Inspector looked at Bridget.

"Yes, we will come together." Bridget was in shock.

"A police car will take you two home, try and get some rest. Then I will see you both tomorrow to give us a statement."

Before leaving to go back to the police station, the Inspector sat in his car. He was thinking about what Miss Weston had just told him about Mr. Hill. He opened up the letter she had handed to him. Did he really not kill Brian Dent? No, he must have, the evidence was there in black and white. It all makes sense, but why lie? He's going to be hanged for what he has done. He has no reason to lie.

CHAPTER SIXTY-TWO

When the police took Sylvia and Bridget home, their street was in darkness. No one knew what had happened to them earlier that evening. Sylvia and Bridget thanked the policeman that had brought them home.

When Sylvia went inside, she went straight upstairs to wake her mum and dad. At first, they thought Sylvia was drunk and talking silly, but when they could see Sylvia was serious, they both jumped out of bed and went downstairs to make a cup of tea.

"Oh, Sylvia I can't believe Johnny has something to do with it, he was such a likeable lad. Whatever made him murder that poor woman?" Sylvia's mum was shocked, but when Sylvia filled her mum and dad in about Johnny, they began to understand. But even more concerned about a murderer still roaming free or was he telling all the truth?

"That war still causing trouble, those Germans!" Sylvia's dad was in the Army and was on the front line in Dunkirk as a Sergeant. He had seen all those men killed, especially on the beach. Sylvia's mum and dad could see Sylvia was in shock, so they told her to go to bed and try and get some rest.

Her parents stayed up a while trying to get a grip on what had happened to Sylvia and Bridget. "I do hope Bridget is alright?" Sylvia's mum wondered. "I will wait till morning and go and see her."

"I bet she be over here if I know Bridget," her husband replied before they both went back to bed for a few hours.

CHAPTER SIXTY-THREE

When Bridget got inside, she went up to her parents' room to wake them up. Just like Sylvia's mum and dad they thought Bridget was drunk and messing around. They couldn't believe this had happened.

"Whatever was going through his mind to do those terrible things?" Bridget's mum was stunned. Bridget then told them all what Johnny had said to them earlier.

"Johnny always seemed a nice lad."

"That's the war for you, it can break a man." Bridget's dad was also in the Army and had seen horrible things. Things you would only see in your worst nightmare.

But her parents could see Bridget was upset.

"I think the worst thing about it is, how one minute Johnny was the nicest man you could meet. He would have given you his last penny. Then to have done all those things." Bridget was finding it hard to accept it and found herself crying.

"You poor thing. Life can be so cruel sometimes."

Bridget cried as her mum tried to comfort her.

"I think you should go to bed and try to get some rest. You will be exhausted by morning," she said as she hugged her daughter.

Bridget nodded "I think I will try and get some sleep. Me and Sylvia have to go to the police station tomorrow."

"Me and your dad will make sure you're up to go."

Bridget went to her bedroom and got into bed, but it was impossible to sleep after all that had happened. She just lay there going over everything. Grieving over someone who wasn't really there, just a pretence. Bridget did wonder if she and Sylvia would ever see their Johnny again? Was it so selfish to think like that, to just forget he existed?

There was just one thing Bridget knew and that was Johnny would be hanged for what he had done. It wasn't fair that she and Sylvia and the folk at work only got to see the nice part of Johnny. When the factory workers heard, they would be slating him. But Bridget knew deep down that Johnny was a killer and that will never change.

CHAPTER SIXTY-FOUR

As Suzi was cooking the breakfast, the news came on the radio.

"Early this morning a man was arrested for the murders of a Mr. Brian Dent and Miss Vera Jones. The man in question is a Mr. Johnny Hill - a local man who works at All Parts in Manchester."

Sid was in the front room playing with the kids, when Suzi came rushing in.

"I can't believe what I just heard on the radio!"

As Sid played with the kids, he became curious to what Suzi had just heard. "What did the news say?"

"You will never guess; Johnny Hill has been arrested for the two murders!" Suzi sat on the sofa in complete shock. The two of them couldn't believe what Suzi just told him. "Of all people I wouldn't think Johnny was the killer, he was always so cheerful, I wonder why he did it?" Suzi sat there shaking her head.

"So did the news say he's been arrested for both murders?"

"Yes, it did. Why you ask?" Suzi questioned Sid.

"I just wondered that's all." Once Suzi went back in the kitchen to finish cooking breakfast, Sid got a thinking. You see, Sid had been keeping a dark secret for weeks now. He hadn't slept properly for a while, not since the murder of Brian Dent.

FLASHBACK

Going back to the 3rd of April - everything was going well up until then. It all started when Brian demanded more money off Sid after he had found out he had been selling parts cheap on the black market.

After Sid thought on it, he decided to have it out with Brian and tell him he wasn't going to sell the parts anymore, but Brian told Sid if he didn't keep selling the parts, he would find himself telling the manager anyway.

So, later that same night, Sid went back to the factory, as he knew Brian worked late most Mondays. Sid thought he would try again and make Brian see sense, that they should stop before they got caught.

But Brian didn't see it like Sid, he started mouthing off at Sid. "If you don't keep selling the parts I will inform Mr. Mortimer!" Sid couldn't understand how, but he lost his temper and hit Brian to the ground.

Sid always carried a pocketknife, not thinking straight, he got it out. Before he knew it, he'd stabbed Brian straight in the heart. He'd panicked and ran and, on the way home, chucked the pocketknife in the river. As he'd hurried home, he was scared someone had seen him run from the factory. Sid wasn't even sure that Brian was dead until the next morning when he went into work.

And now Johnny will be charged for Brian's murder. It looked like Sid had gotten away with it. The Inspector would not believe Johnny when he tells him that he didn't kill Brian, not with all the killing Johnny had done.

As with the Rat poison that was found in Mr Brian Dent's body after the autopsy someone had been putting the rat poison in his cup of tea each day for the last three weeks. Just small amounts at first. You see, Mr Dent always had his break at 4 o'clock on the dot. That one person was waiting for their move, each day. Someone who hated Brian just as much as the others did. This person wasn't evil, they just wanted Brian to stop black mailing them or, in a strange way, teach him a lesson.

Each day, Annie Bright would take the packer's slips to Mr Dent's office. Annie was so desperate to keep her secret from her friends and family she would sneak into the stock room and take a small amount of rat poison, then put it in a bag, ready to put in Brian's drink. Clearly Annie wasn't thinking straight. Brian Dent was the cause of Annie doing this terrible act. Now luck had it the Inspector would never know where the rat poison came from.

CHAPTER SIXTY-FIVE

By the morning, Sylvia was feeling low. She hadn't got much sleep thinking about Johnny. Especially knowing there could still be a murderer out there somewhere. She thought, I bet all the folk at the factory would have heard about it by now. It was like talking about someone else, not the Johnny she knew. Would she ever see Johnny again? All this was going around Sylvia's mind.

Once she was up, she washed and changed, then went to have some breakfast.

In the kitchen her mum was cooking bacon and eggs. "So, did you try and get some sleep?" she asked Sylvia.

"Not much. I just kept thinking what will happen to Johnny now?"

"Try not to think about that just now, else it will eat you up." Sylvia knew her Mum was right. "There's tea in the pot, pour yourself one." After listening to her Mum, Sylvia got up and gave her a hug. "Whatever was that for? Not that I'm complaining or anything."

"I just want you to know I appreciate what you do for me." Sylvia knew her mum would help her make sense of it all. After Sylvia had her breakfast, she was feeling a lot better than she was earlier.

"Do you and Bridget want me and your dad to take you to the police station?"

"I'm not sure, I will see what Bridget wants to do first, then I will get back to you. Is that alright with you Mum?"

"No, that will be just fine."

"I'm going over to see Bridget now, won't be long," Sylvia said to her Mum.

When Sylvia got to Bridget's house, she knocked on the door. Sylvia didn't have to wait long until someone answered it. Luckily it was Bridget, who put her arms around Sylvia. "I take it you're glad to see me?"

Bridget laughed at Sylvia: she always said the right thing. "Come into the kitchen, Sylvia!" Bridget's mum shouted.

When Sylvia went into the kitchen there was Bridget's mum, dad and brother, Derick. "Would you like a cup of tea?" Bridget's mum asked Sylvia.

"Oh yes please, Mrs. Molt."

"Please, call me Sarah! We were so shocked when Bridget told us last night. You poor things, having to go through that. Who would have thought Johnny could do those terrible things, he always seemed to be jolly? It shows you can't trust anyone. Oh, and to think there's someone still out there who is a killer too!"

"Pete's sake woman, let the girl alone, she doesn't want you chatting away at her." Bridget's dad said, winking his eye at Sylvia before turning his attention back to the paper.

"I bet your mum and dad were shocked weren't they, Sylvia?"

"Yes, they were, but I was glad they were there for me."

"I bet you were." Bridget's mum sighed.

Bridget asked Sylvia to come up to her bedroom. "I've had that all morning; they're driving me potty," Bridget moaned to Sylvia. "I know, they are just trying to help, but they can be too much sometimes."

"I know how you feel, Mum and Dad can be like that. It's 10.30 now, it will take us 15 minutes on the bus, to get to the police station."

"So shall we catch the 11.20? It'll drop us off right outside the police station."

"That will give us plenty of time to get a coffee before we go in." Bridget was happy with the plan.

After Sylvia said goodbye to Bridget's mum and dad, she went back to her house to get ready for when Bridget called for her. "So, what did Bridget have to say?" Sylvia's mum asked.

"We are going to the police station on the bus now."

"That's fine, long as we know." When She was ready, there was a knock on the door. When Sylvia answered, it was Bridget.

"I'm off now Mum, see you later," Sylvia shouted to her mum as she went through the door.

As Sylvia and Bridget walked to the bus stop, they both were starting to get nervous, both lighting a cigarette and trying not to think about it.

215

"At least the bus has turned up on time." Bridget gave a faint smile as she put her cigarette out.

While on the bus, Sylvia and Bridget never spoke a word - both were thinking about the night before and what a good day they had with Gregg and Ben at the football match. Sylvia or Bridget hadn't really been thinking about Gregg or Ben since last night.

"I'm going to hate going to work tomorrow with all the questions, it's going to be hell," Bridget moaned.

"Or shall we take a few days off work?" Sylvia thinking out loud.

"Let's see what Inspector Wright says first." They both agreed.

When the bus reached their stop, they get off and walked to the police station, they were 30 minutes early, so they went in the canteen for a coffee. After ordering two coffees they went and sat down. Not saying a word, like they were waiting to go for an important interview. When they finished their coffees, they both made their way to Inspector Wright's office.

As Sylvia and Bridget got nearer, their hearts started to beat faster. When they got there, PC Green asked them to take a seat. After a few minutes, the Inspector came out from his office.

"Thank you for coming, I know it must be difficult for you both, could you please come with me?" Walking down the corridor Sylvia and Bridget were very nervous by now. "Please both, take a seat. As you know, Mr. Johnny Hill has admitted to both murders, and has been charged. Not mentioning all the murders of the Jews in Germany and Poland. Mr. Jim West's statement, the letter you found, and both your statements will be enough to charge Mr. Hill with the murders."

They both looked at each other in disbelief. They both felt so disheartened that the man they called their best friend was truly a cold-blooded killer. At least they hadn't got to worry about a murderer being on the loose now.

After Sylvia and Bridget gave their statements to the Inspector he said, "We may even be able to charge him with Mr Bobby Bentley's murder in London two years ago."

Sylvia and Bridget looked at each other. Inspector Wright could see by their faces they didn't know about the murder of Mr Bobby Bentley. "Did you not know about this murder Mr Hill did?"

Sylvia spoke first, "No, we didn't."

"Well, it was when Mr Hill lived in London, he killed him because Mr Bentley had a photo of him when he was a Nazi Officer. That is the reason why he murdered him. Before now the case was left open till now."

Sylvia and Bridget were surprised Johnny never mentioned it the night before. Who else had he killed? The Inspector could see they were both confused with it all.

"Will you be asking us to be witnesses?" Sylvia was concerned.

"Well, that depends if Mr Hill pleads guilty in court. Have you any questions?"

"Will he be hanged?" Sylvia asked.

"Yes, he will, if he is found guilty."

Bridget then asked the Inspector, "If it goes to court, how long 'til he goes?"

"Well, it depends on how much evidence we can get against him, there's the photo from Mr. Jim West, so there's grounds there for him to murder for it so as to keep it a secret. Also, Mr West's statement. Then there's the letter you gave me last night, along with both your statements. All strong evidence."

"We can't believe he helped to gas those people in Poland and Germany. He was a likeable and caring person to us; how can someone one minute be nice, then do those murders?" Sylvia expecting an answer from the Inspector.

"Surprisingly, evil people do keep things from the innocent. Why they do these evil things, who knows. I will let you know if you need to come back into the station again. Or if you need to get in touch with me do not hesitate to call me. Well, I think that is everything."

As soon as Sylvia and Bridget left the Inspector's office, they rushed out of the police station. When they caught the next bus home, they both couldn't believe Johnny never told them about the murder in London.

It made Sylvia and Bridget wonder who else had he killed. Never mind the Jews, it was too horrible to think about. To think all this time, they were friends with a natural born killer.

Printed in Great Britain
by Amazon

74677734R00127